HIKIKOMORI AND THE RENTAL SISTER

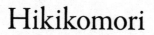

Hikikomori

AND THE

Rental Sister

A NOVEL

JEFF BACKHAUS

HarperCollins*PublishersLtd*

Published by HarperCollins Publishers Ltd, by arrangement with Algonquin Books of
Chapel Hill, a division of Workman Publishing Company, Inc., New York.

First Canadian edition

HarperCollins Publishers Ltd
2 Bloor Street East, 20th Floor
Toronto, Ontario, Canada
M4W 1A8

www.harpercollins.ca

Library and Archives Canada Cataloguing in Publication
Backhaus, Jeff
Hikikomori and the rental sister / Jeff Backhaus.

ISBN 978-1-44341-800-3

I. Title.
PS3602.A347H55 2012   813'.6   C2012-905913-7

Design by Anne Winslow

Printed in the United States of America
RRD 9 8 7 6 5 4 3 2 1

HIKIKOMORI AND THE RENTAL SISTER

One

I AM CROUCHED IN THE darkness behind my bedroom door, listening for my wife to crack the silence with a sneeze or cough or some other little noise that tells me it's not safe to leave. She is down the hall, in the room meant for children, and I know she leaves her door open, and that her ears never sleep, that they listen for my exit noises, the retracting dead bolt and creaking floorboards. Heart without peace, she might just be lying in bed awake, holding her breath. A river of sweat flows down my spine and pools between my legs, but I cannot move, not until I'm sure she won't hear me slinking out.

With two fingers and a thumb I turn my dead bolt. The sound seems to shake the entire apartment. Next, slowly, the knob lock. When the echoes finally subside and the silence returns, I pull open the door just enough to peer down the hall. The greasy odor of Chinese food spills in, her lonely dinner, probably left open on the counter and already beginning to spoil, the winter flies laying their eggs. Leaving food out overnight used to be a no-no.

My eyes adjust to the shadows, and I look down the hall and into the living room. Streetlight gleams through the windows, folding over the arm of the sofa, wrapping around the lampshade, but I see no movement, no human silhouette. On the left, her door is open. I watch and listen for another quarter hour or so. Hard to tell how long.

Sometimes she detects my exit, not passively, not the way you detect a hint of guilt in your lover's eyes, no, she ambushes me, and her weapons are pleas and tears and wild, girlish punches. So, the vigilance and the crouching.

It's time. I grab my sneakers and stand up and zip my heavy winter jacket. The pooled sweat runs down my thigh. I slip out of my timeless cocoon and into the hallway and close the door behind me, silently untwisting the knob. If my wife wakes up while I'm out, she'll see my door is closed, as normal, and she won't pause to investigate. She'll empty her bladder or swallow a cool drink and go back to bed.

I should stoop low here and quickly pass her door out of sight, but

I can never manage it. Standing upright I look into her room. She is sleeping, weighed down by a thick wool blanket, which I bought for her—for us—one cool autumn weekend at the beach. Her hair has spilled onto the pillow in long, gentle waves, and I remember the nights when I lay in that luxurious spot, the scent of her hair lulling me to sleep. My left hand begins to quiver, waves of pain and regret. I dare not linger.

I creep into the kitchen. The open containers of Chinese food are sitting on the table. Wrappers, chopsticks, an unfolded fortune. I consider throwing the containers away and cleaning up the mess for her, but too much time and noise and I don't want to spook her.

Through the dark living room, past the old upright piano and into the entryway. Every floorboard squeaks, a little or a lot. I move quickly. I place my loosely tied sneakers on the floor and slip in my feet. My hand has settled, the waves have receded. I step out of the apartment and into the fifth-floor hallway. It's quiet, but my neighbor might be spying on me, eye to the door.

Down the stairs, out the double front doors, and I am outside, in the world. The blast of raw winter air is refreshing. I wonder if the sweat in my beard has frozen. I suck in air through my nose, and it feels like the totality of winter's cold is concentrated in my nostrils. After a shiver I push the air out my mouth—warm now—an evanescent cloud.

Up and down the block, no people, just a row of frozen, lifeless

cars and dirty snow piled up along the sidewalk, a little gray mountain range. The streetlamps impart an icy glow, not so much illumi-
nating as casting long, thick shadows, making the street somehow
darker. Apartment blocks rise above me along both sides of the
street, and all the windows are black and I imagine the people inside sleeping, warm in their beds. While they sleep I walk, which
after another month in my room is no longer automatic. My arms
aren't supposed to swing so far, I know, and I struggle to find a natural rhythm.

I turn a corner and another and up ahead on 107th Street a vagrant sleeps on the sidewalk, his back against the wall, legs straight
out, feet splayed. Resting against his stomach sits a piece of torn
cardboard on which, in black letters, he has scratched an indecipher-
able plea. A stained paper cup has fallen out of his leathery hand, a
few coins scattered about. His crotch is soaked and he sits in a pool
of foul liquid. A bolt of empathy strikes me as I remember that, if
not for my wife, I might be the one sleeping there on the freezing
sidewalk.

I look closely at the vagrant's chest. At first I'm not sure, I wait
and watch some more, and then I finally see it, so slight, the up and
down, the breathing. Life, air, in and out. Soaked in piss, still a man.
He will eventually wake up and go about his day. He will repulse
people. They will give him wide berth so as not to inhale his stink.

I walk on. A taxicab drives past, the passenger's head slumped against the window. Even now, in deepest, coldest night, certain people move from place to place. After a left turn I spot the friendly blue awning on the corner at the opposite end of the block. Pristine white light from the convenience store floods the sidewalk and rolls into the street, a simple and defiant patch of brilliance amid the darkness.

The automatic glass doors slide open, and the cashier perks up from behind the counter. He gives me that look every time. I doubt any other customer gets that look. It's reserved for me, the man who comes in every few weeks to stock up, always in the dead of night, always alone. The cashier doesn't know me from my life three years ago; as far as he's concerned I have always been this way, sneaking into the store, stocking up, retreating.

I know what the cashier is thinking. He's imagining what I am in the weeks between my shopping sprees: serial killer, pedophile, kidnapper, or terrorist cooking up bombs in the basement. Maybe tonight he picks one and runs with it, kidnapper perhaps, and so in his mind my supplies, the frozen dinners, aren't for me but my captive. Not bombs in the basement but a prisoner, a woman, or more likely a girl. So into the store at four in the morning walks a kidnapping pedophile shopping for food and supplies to keep his prey just barely alive. But the cashier won't call the cops. As far as he's concerned, I'm only shopping. The rest is none of his business.

I know what people think of me. Except that nobody thinks of me, because there is no reason to think of me, because I live apart, because I have locked out the world.

I grab two red plastic baskets and head for the aisles. Frozen turkey dinners, frozen waffles, dried soups, ramen, macaroni and cheese, butter. Saltines and a block of cheddar. Canned peaches and string beans. Canned chicken. Canned ravioli, which my son loved and I hated, yet now I eat it. I take the full baskets to the counter and set them down, but my shopping is not finished. I head to the magazine rack.

He watches me pick out magazines, with his own eyes now, but he has been watching me the entire time, as I strolled up and down the aisles. There are cameras throughout the store, and I know the monitors are behind the counter.

I bring the magazines to the counter, where he has already begun scanning my frozen dinners across the red laser beams, a synthetic ping heralding success, a congratulations of sorts and probably the only encouragement he gets all night.

I pay in cash. No need for him to know my name. I have my own money, though money—the issue of money—hangs over me always. My supply isn't that of a working man, replenished every two weeks, topped off; my supply is finite, leftover savings, a stash. I say nothing as the cashier bags my groceries and magazines. I don't look him in the eye.

The automatic glass doors slide open and I step outside, underneath the friendly blue awning, and then back down the block, plastic grocery bags looped heavy around my wrists, biting into my skin. Snow has begun to fall, making the sidewalk slick. From time to time a flake melts on my face. An icy sting, then a warm trickle.

The vagrant still sits against the wall. He's dusted white with snowcover, like a pile of garbage. I set down my bags and pick up his paper cup, fixing it upright on the sidewalk, then I dig into my pocket, pull out the change from my groceries, and drop the coins into the cup. But it's so cold tonight, and he's covered with snow, there must be a better place to sleep, over a steam grate, in a shelter, or even at the bottom of an empty stairwell, a little closer to the warm earth.

I kick his foot, just a tap, just to wake him. No response. Again, harder this time. Still no response. I bend down closer to get a good look at his chest, to look for the up and down. But I can't be certain.

I give him another kick, a big one. "Wake up, it's snowing."

"What the hell?" he says, trying to focus his eyes.

"It's snowing."

"Who the fuck are you? Get away!"

He pulls his hood over his head and draws it closed around his face. I loop the grocery bags around my wrists and walk on.

Back at my apartment building I climb the seven steps to the front door but I do not enter. Not yet. I set the bags down and sit on the top step, facing out toward the street. My warmth melts the snow and my jeans soak it up.

In a few hours the sun will rise behind the clouds, a gray morning, and the lights will come on one by one, and people will come out and sweep off their steps and warm up their cars and scrape their windshields. But for now everyone is still asleep. My wife is still asleep in what used to be our son's room. I make a fist of my quivering left hand and watch my breath cloud up and disappear into the darkness.

Two

THE PATTER OF HIS little feet echoes against the hallway walls, so much motion, so little movement, a child's untamed gait. He knocks on my door. "Daddy?"

His sweet voice, my precious revenant back to visit me, but I cannot let him in. His dark eyes looking up at mine: unbearable. There is no evading a child's sharp, innocent glance.

But it couldn't be my boy knocking at the door. That's impossible. Where is my mind? It's Silke, my wife, who knocks. She tells me she made eggs for breakfast, and that she made too much and that I can have the rest if I want. I hear her set a plate on the floor outside my door and, after a pause, her retreating footfalls. The front door opens, then closes.

Food at the door is her simplest gambit, naïve and—in its own little way—heartbreaking. But I know she may have closed the door without leaving and taken off her shoes and tiptoed back to the end of the hall. My interaction with the world is all zigging and zagging, the communication of avoidance, a dance of great feeling and intricate steps: signals and sounds, interpreted and acted upon this way and that.

The coffee's fragrance is still lingering from her breakfast. In happier times she woke me up with that coffee, she welcomed me home with that coffee, she kept me alert with that coffee during late nights working. She tried teaching me more than once how to make it. I could never get it right. But now the coffee and its fragrance is just a reminder of how one Saturday morning I destroyed our family. It's not her fault; to her the coffee is mere routine, a necessary jumpstart to her day. I'm sure she has no idea that each cup renews my guilt.

Sometimes she does not come home at night and in the morning there is no coffee scent. Business trips, probably. No way to be sure. Sometimes I hear the luggage wheels, sometimes I don't. Days and weeks with the apartment to myself. But even then I stay behind my dead bolt.

She must be gone by now, it's safe to get the eggs. I once thought of installing a peephole but all she'd have to do is cover the lens with a piece of tape and I'd be as blind as before and she'd have gained a little victory over me.

I have turned sour, it's true, and scared and scarred, but there is a certain destiny to life, and I know what viciousness I'm capable of. So, I've stopped time. The future will never come. I've tried explaining it to Silke, through the door a long time ago, that she and we and the world would all be better off with me in here, but she doesn't believe it. She refuses to believe it.

When I was young I asked my mother what happens after you die. "If you're good you go to heaven," she said.

"Then what?"

"That's it."

"But what comes after heaven?"

"Nothing, heaven is forever," she said, and I left the room satisfied, but then I thought for a bit and came back and Mom was folding laundry.

"So it never stops," I said, "it just keeps going and going and going?"

She smiled and nodded and I'm sure she meant it as comfort but the concept of forever terrified me. Too big to wrap my little head around, heaven sounded like hell.

When Mom died, Dad continued on, alone. He did not throw me away and start over. Surely he saw his wife in me, but he shed no tears. And his fortitude, his mettle and grit, and his benevolence, they ended with him. My dad did not bequeath me with the same; he forgot about my inheritance, or he always meant to give it to me but lost his chance, because one day in spring he went out to get the mail and on his way back—halfway between the mailbox and the front door—he fell to the concrete, a heart attack. He was wearing his bathrobe and held a handful of utility bills. Just like that.

In the casket he had his hands folded on his chest. He was perfectly still. He looked exactly like me. I was looking at my own funeral, ahead in time, when some unseen voice shouts: Tessler family! Everyone move one spot to the right! Grandpa, you're in the grave now. Thomas, you get in the casket. Little Tessler Boy, you're in the hot seat now, and pay attention, because you're next.

I think my mom came down to get my dad. I think she was lonely up there in endless heaven.

The eggs are cold but delicious. Apparently she made too much toast, too, and spread it with my favorite strawberry-rhubarb jam. I am not used to fresh eggs: soon I'll be sick. But for now they are delicious. I wash the plate in my bathroom sink and set it on the hallway floor.

I have sat cross-legged on my bed and read all the books by all the major physicists, so I am well acquainted with the concept of time as we currently understand it, and a tenuous understanding it is, for nobody seems to know quite what time is and whether it flows or only appears to flow, whether it has a beginning or an end, whether it can be stopped, and whether there are gaps between moments, and if so, what those gaps might be.

My television is on, but I don't watch it. I find a show with a peaceful rhythm—baseball game, soap opera, courtroom drama—and put the volume on low and go about my business. The best days are the courtroom-drama marathon days, when I can set the channel and leave it there all day and be soothed by the pleas of the guilty and innocent. My television is like a metronome, so I can march in place forever, a beating heart to tell me I'm still alive.

I wake up in the dark, above the covers, television flickering in my face. I hear the last gurgles of her flushing toilet. She is home.

From in the hall she says, "I see you liked your eggs."

I point my head toward the door. "I ate my eggs." My voice sounds foreign to me. All day long thoughts flow like torrents but words never escape, and now here they are, like worms falling out of my mouth.

"You ate them but you didn't enjoy them?" she says.

"I ate them and I enjoyed them."

"You could say thank you."

"Thank you." She is chatty tonight, and her words slur together, as though her sentences are one long word.

"Too much salt?"

"Salt?"

"Were the eggs too salty?"

"No, they were perfectly salted." I regret opening my mouth, words and worms. Nothing comes out right.

"What about pepper?"

"Did you come here to talk about salt and pepper?"

She doesn't answer, but she doesn't leave. She knows better than to try the knob. She pushes the empty plate aside, and in the slit beneath the door are two shadows, her feet, just standing there. Life flows smoother when she doesn't come down the hallway, when she doesn't talk to me—or when I have the sense not to respond. Yet she stays, yet she comes down the hall, yet she believes in me. She thinks I'm the same man she married. And maybe I am, and maybe that's the problem, that I always have been this man and always will be.

"Don't you want to know where I've been all night?" she asks.

"It's late," I say, "maybe you should go to bed."

"I'm not tired." The two shadows move, and I hear her back slide down the wall and the dull thud of her ass landing on the floor. Even after so long, there are still things to learn about my wife. I search for meaning in every sound through the door. Her voice these days is different. More urgent. "You're not even curious . . ." she says.

"You should go to bed. It's late."

"I should go to bed. It's late. Is that right? You think you know what I should do?"

A far-off siren floats into my room. Someone out there is having an emergency, someone is life or death. I squeeze my left hand into a fist.

"Don't you want to know?"

"Are you sure you want to tell me?" I ask. "Are you sure you want me to know what you've been doing?"

No hesitation, hardly a pause, and the brutal sound of plate colliding with door rips through the apartment. The shattered pieces ricochet off the walls and crash to the floor. Then there is silence.

Hours later, when I am sure she is asleep, I open the door, collect all the shards and take them into my room. My acrimony is sharp and real but it dies in a flash and I'm left with only deep remorse that starts at my core and eats its way to my skin, where it sits and chews, a constant, burning sorrow that she doesn't realize exists—my bitterness is all she knows anymore—which makes the sorrow burn even hotter, and on and on it spirals.

Three

A T 9:55 A.M., MEGUMI steps onto the floor of the Hamamoto Wagashi Boutique. She leans over to Naoko. "You feel as shitty as I do?"

"Worse," Naoko says.

"My throat still tastes like beer and squid."

"Mine still tastes like that white guy."

"You went home with him?"

Hamamoto appears from the back room. "Good morning, girls," she says. She is taller than Megumi and wears a tight cerulean dress with her hair pulled back, smoky makeup shading her sharp eyes. She looks young, unless you look really close, and every day Megumi wishes a little wish that she, too, will look as beautiful as Hamamoto when she's that old.

"Megumi, I want you to make room in the case on the middle shelf for the new *tsuyaguri* we're getting in today."

"Better than last time, I hope."

"Let's try it together when it comes in and if it's good enough you can make a nice countertop display."

Hamamoto examines the display cases to make sure the delicate *wagashi* are perfectly arranged. Cakes, cookies, jellies, everything is in order. She pulls up the blinds, flips the sign, and unlocks the door. Ten a.m. exactly. Midnight back home.

After a time, while Megumi is squatting behind the display case polishing a spot for the new shipment of tsuyaguri, the first customer of the morning walks in from the cold, a blond woman, seemingly tall, but from Megumi's low angle down by the floor it's hard to tell. Hamamoto comes out to greet the woman. Megumi watches through the display case glass. It looks like the woman has stumbled into the wrong place. She doesn't have the typical wide-eyed giddiness at being suddenly surrounded by all things delicious, and in fact she doesn't look at the colorful wagashi at all. Her smile is forced and there is shame in her eyes.

Megumi shifts her squat to get a better angle through the glass.

Hamamoto gives the blond customer a slight bow, basically just a polite nod of the head, since foreigners never know what to do with a real bow. Megumi can't make out what they're saying, but just from the tone she knows this must be the one they've been waiting for. The one she never thought would actually come. The woman's hands are for a few moments clasped between Hamamoto's. She's younger than Megumi expected. The woman follows Hamamoto behind the counter, where they disappear into the back room.

Megumi stands up. Her head pounds from last night's beer and sake. Naoko gives her a confused look, but Megumi just shrugs. She steps outside for some fresh air.

The winter morning tightens the skin on her face. The sun peeks through holes in the passing clouds, thick and heavy as though they are about to burst with snow. A cold breeze lifts and twists her hair, sending strands into her face, but she doesn't brush them away.

Across Minetta Street is a small wedge of park, just enough space for a narrow path, a couple of frozen benches, some overgrown bushes and trees, among them a single cherry. She wonders if Hamamoto chose this location for her shop because of the cherry tree or if she even sneaked in long ago and planted it herself. Now the tree is just a frozen black skeleton, but in springtime it blooms like a proud pink beacon. How sad, she thinks, this beautiful tree in such a small space next to trees that do not bloom, trapped by streets and traffic, breathing fumes, choking. Just then the breeze blows chilly air onto her scalp.

The door opens. "It's time," Hamamoto says. "Let's go."

But Megumi doesn't move. "I listened," she says, "but I never agreed." She can get away with talking like that only because she is in New York, and not Japan. She didn't come all the way here to act like she's still at home.

"Let's sit," Hamamoto says, grabbing Megumi's arm. She pulls her across the street. They sit next to each other in the park, on one of the wooden benches. They are alone. A patch of sky opens up and sunlight strikes the concrete, but then it is gone and the park goes gray. "If you were having second thoughts, you should have told me sooner."

"Why does it have to be me? Naoko could—"

"Naoko wouldn't stand a chance."

Megumi blows on her hands. The cherry tree slices the breeze. It whistles.

"You're the only one who knows what it's like," Hamamoto says.

"I'm trying to forget."

"It's a chance to put to use everything you learned from your brother."

"I learned that if I set birthday presents outside his door, they will sit there for days and days and never get opened. How should I put that to use?" Those presents are probably still sitting on the shelf in her old bedroom in Tokyo, behind the vase, wrapped, waiting, collecting dust.

"Her husband needs our help."

"I never heard of an American *hikikomori*. Americans don't get quieter, they get louder. They go crazy and start shooting everyone."

"That's exactly why he needs us. This country doesn't know what to do with him."

"But I'm not a rental sister."

"There's nobody else. He's not back home, he's here. It doesn't matter if you're not perfect—you're all there is, all he has. All she has."

An old man enters the park, pulling a small, wheeled suitcase. The suitcase is dented and stained. The straps are frayed. One of the wheels is locked. It scrapes against the concrete. His face has a large scab. The crust is yellow. His mittens are brand new. He lies on a bench. His sneakers have no laces.

"When I heard about them, I could've kept quiet. I could have kept eating my arugula salad, but I stuck my neck out and said we could help. I gave my word."

"Why didn't you ask me first?"

"Because time is always running out. And because I knew you would do the right thing."

With cold fingertips Megumi presses her temples. She sucks in the wintry air. Maybe her vocal cords will go brittle and crack.

"Megumi, I need an answer."

"It was different with my brother. I wouldn't know where to begin."

"She's up in my office right now, waiting."

"It's not fair."

"What should I tell her?"

"Tell her I can't do it." The empty park swallows her refusal. There are no lingering echoes. The old man does not stir.

"If that's your decision, you're going to have to tell her yourself. You'll have to look her in the eye and tell her you won't help."

She could quit. She could walk out of the park and down the cold street and never come back, she could just walk and walk, away, alone.

"Don't you wish someone would've been there to help your brother?" Megumi's arm twitches, her hand flies open, she nearly slaps Hamamoto across the face. Not because she's wrong, but because she is exploiting the fact that the heart's sorest spot is also its softest. "By the way, about it being different from your brother, you're right. It's worse."

"I'm supposed to ask how it's worse."

"Imagine it wasn't your brother. Imagine it was your husband."

"I don't get it."

"She's putting up a brave front in there. But time is always running out."

The old man on the bench coughs. He doesn't put his hand to his mouth or press his chest. He just coughs into the winter morning, as though coughing is breathing.

"Hama-*neesan,* I'm sorry."

"It's just talking. All you'd have to do is go to his door and talk. If it doesn't work out—if there's something bad about him—you can stop. But first you have to try. Please."

"I'm sorry."

Hamamoto doesn't go with her; she stays on the bench. As Megumi is about to cross the street, Hamamoto calls her over to the fence. "Tell Silke I apologize. Tell her good luck."

Megumi climbs the narrow staircase to the loft office. She steps lightly, but the stairs still creak. Silke's pretty green eyes are bloodshot.

At the side table she prepares two cups of tea, pouring hot water from an electric kettle. The water steams. Her movements are not steady. She holds the tray with both hands and sets it between them on Hamamoto's desk. The room is sparsely furnished, windowless, a soft yellow glow from two floor lamps in opposite corners. In the heavy, undisturbed silence, the outside world seems far away. Silke presses her mouth into a tight smile. But then it's gone.

"These cups are over one hundred years old," Megumi says. Foreigners never understand the significance, but she says it anyway. It's not that the age itself is important or that one hundred years is particularly old, but that for one hundred years people have been sitting across from each other drinking tea out of these same cups, a long string of moments that have come and gone never to return, and in that whole time the only thing that hasn't changed is the cups.

"What kind of tea is it?"

"*Hojicha*. Gently roasted green tea from a special shop in Kyoto."

"I've never been to Japan." She takes a sip. Americans have such large mouths.

"It's a beautiful country. But, Mrs. Tessler, I'm afraid that Hamamoto was a little pre . . . prema — "

"Premature?"

"I'm sorry. My boss was a little premature with you." Silke's blood-shot eyes burrow into hers, into her head, downward, through the knot in her throat, all the way to her stomach. She sickens. She knows Silke's expression. She, too, wore it, when her brother was a hikikomori. Her mother wore it. Her father wore it worst of all. Fear. Shame. Hopelessness. And something else, too: exhaustion. No matter when, no matter where, that person alone in his room never left their minds. In a way, he wasn't missing at all, he wasn't withdrawn. He was stuck in their brains, pounding their skulls with his fist. Every dream fell into a nightmare.

"Your English is very good. How long have you been here?"

"I thank my father for my English. He spoke English at his job, and he thought foreign language was so important. Every day when he came home from work — even if it was late — he made me tell him about my day, using English only. Fifteen minutes, every day. I hated it at first, but now . . ."

"All I have is a couple years of high school French."

"Je m'appelle Megumi," she says with an exaggerated accent, arching her eyebrow, trying to coax a smile.

"You speak French, too?" There is no smile.

"A little. And Korean. But I've never been to France, so I'm not a good speaker."

Silke doesn't savor her tea. She sips like she's smoking a cigarette at an interrogation, and she can't sit quite still, little shifts back and forth, side to side, like she's in the midst of swirling winds.

Her father's expression seemed normal outside, but at home, as he chewed his rice, as he thumbed through the newspaper, his eyes would not focus. And if a stray sound leaked from her brother's room, they'd all turn their heads and freeze, like a family of deer in the meadow, alert for what comes next. But nothing came next. Only silence. They went back to their newspaper or television or homework.

What does Silke do when she hears a stray sound from her husband's room? Does she tilt her head, perk up her ears, cry? And when no more sound slips out, what activity does she return to, what fills her empty hours?

"Premature?" Silke asks.

The day is too cold, the air too bitter and merciless to send this woman outside with no hope, with only fear and exhaustion. "I just meant that I'm afraid I can't help you unless I know a little more about you and your husband." Just a few questions, Megumi thinks, a few questions before she decides.

Silke looks around the room. She squeezes her own shoulder. The air is perfectly still. The tea no longer steams.

"How long has he been withdrawn?"

Now Silke's body goes quiet. She sits still and takes a slow sip of tea. "It's been three years."

"And does he ever come out to see you?"

"Never."

"And do you ever go into his room?"

"I'm afraid."

"Why are you afraid?"

"I'm sorry. I shouldn't have said that."

When they were growing up, she and her brother slept together on the floor, on the same futon, next to their parents on their big futon. Their apartment had only one room. Sometimes, in the dark, when they thought she and her brother were asleep, her mom and dad's futon would rustle. They were all so close then. When years later their apartment had six rooms, though, she became afraid to enter or even look into her brother's room. Afraid of what she might find. Afraid to upset the balance.

"Do you have an idea about why he's in his room?"

"It's because—"

"No no no, not the actual reason, just if you think you know what the reason is."

"I *am* his wife."

"Of course you are."

"But why don't you want to know?"

"Sometimes the reasons aren't what we think they are. So I'll make like he's a friend I'm getting to know. A blank slate. Better chance of getting him out."

"A friend . . . not . . . a brother?"

Megumi understands Silke's meaning. "Yes," she says, "brother. Brother and friend."

"Maybe this is a bad idea." Silke's eyes dart toward the door.

"But don't you want him out?" Her tide is turning. These green eyes are pulling her out to sea.

Silke sets down her cup and kneads her hands together as though numb. "It's been so long. . . . I don't know how it got this way. It's embarrassing."

"You aren't alone, Mrs. Tessler."

Silke stares into her teacup. "Are you sure about that?" she says.

She is so young, barely thirty, Megumi guesses, thirty to her own twenty-two. They are silent for a time. Silke reaches for her teacup but then puts her hands on her lap. "He was such a nice guy. An amazing guy. If he wasn't, I'd have never . . . everything was fine, really, we were happy . . . I just don't want you to think he's a bad guy. He's not a bad guy."

"I'm sure he's wonderful," Megumi says. Silke gives her an odd look. Megumi knows her words don't always come out right. She considers them for a moment before trying again. "The fact that you're here right now proves he's a good guy," she says, and the odd look disappears.

"But to be honest, Me-g—"

"Megumi."

"Megumi. To be honest, I don't know who's behind that door. Is he still . . . see, that's the thing: I need to know who's in there. At this point I can't just stay living like this, but—maybe this sounds crazy—but I can't just leave yet, either."

"It's not crazy."

"Not that I'm blameless, I'm not saying that, but . . . do you understand? And not that he's perfect, but I can't just abandon him, not until I know who's in there. And even then, I don't know, because . . . how did I let things go so far? It's scary how good you get at covering it up. Lies, excuses . . . until it's completely natural and you don't even think you're lying anymore."

"I understand, trust me I do. I've been there. But you're doing the right thing."

Again Silke presses her mouth into a smile. Megumi notices that for the first time Silke is looking at her in the comparative way women look at other women. There is silence for a time, and they both take long drinks of tea.

"What is it, exactly, that you would do?" Silke asks.

"Very simple. You give me a key, I go to your home, I go to his room, I spend time with him." On such a biting day, nobody deserves to be sent away without hope. One visit, that's all. She'll go to him once, and if anything isn't right, she'll never go back. It's too cold to promise anything less.

"Spend time?" She shifts in her seat.

"Talk. I talk to him. And listen."

"What if he doesn't want to talk to you? He hardly ever talks."

"They want to live in their room forever and be left alone. They don't want me coming around, but that doesn't matter, because I won't stop coming." It could be a lie, but it's a lie she needs to hear.

"How often?"

"Maybe once or twice a week at first. All depends on how he responds."

"Does it work?"

Before the teacup reaches her lips she sets it down. "All I can say is that after three years in his room, not much else is going to work. Not if you want things back to normal. The way they were." Silke's eyes are big and round and sad, like two spent stars, their final flicker before going dark and inert forever. Those two spent stars start crying. She expects Silke's crying to grow into sobbing, bawling even, but quiet tears are all she has left, no energy for anything more. "You want him back," she says, wearing a gentle expression. "You want to see him and you want your life back, it's natural. But he's been in there for so long, your husband probably doesn't know *how* to come out of his room. So long that he's not sure if he knows how to live out here anymore."

From the desk drawer she takes a stationery set. For a few minutes she writes, then folds the paper and seals it inside an envelope. "Give him this," she says.

That night she has a hard time falling asleep. She lies on the floor on her futon, searching through the darkness for the web of cracks in the plaster ceiling, all the time seeing the image of Silke Tessler's green eyes glittering with tears. She thinks of Thomas Tessler, unseen Thomas, somewhere out there, all alone in his room, perhaps at this very moment reading her letter, thinking about her as she thinks about him.

Four

ENTIRE AFTERNOONS GO MISSING. I sit cross-legged on the bed or on the floor reading magazines, sometimes unfolding and melting into supine sleep, but sleep is not what steals the hours. They go missing while I am awake, wide awake, so wide that I am rendered unaware. The walls of my room, what tricks they play: boxing in my wilted soul, paralyzing the clock then suddenly lurching it forward hours, even days. Sometimes weeks. Months.

My walls are not completely solid, not without two weaknesses, window and door. Through the window there are trees and buildings and cars and children playing and even the sun arcing through the sky, but I see none of those things, as I keep the shade pulled down to the sill, always. The door separates and connects. It is flimsy, but one day with drill and screwdriver I fortified it with a thick dead bolt, so strong that the door will rip off its hinges before the lock gives way.

My window shade burns golden with the day's last sunrays. Were I to raise the shade, what a sight I'd see, what a crisp winter sunset.

The front door slams. She returns after a hard day at the skyscraper office. Her high heels click through the living room and down the hall to her room. I am not the pet, the dog in its cage waiting for Master's return to be let out, to run in circles and jump and bite: I am the dog that has been digging holes in the lawn, the one who can't raise his eyes. I move to the door to listen.

She talks to me from the hallway. I learn about her day, about the bitter weather and her chapped lips and asshole boss. Quaint concerns. There is nothing new. She talks to the door, not to me. I do not respond. She asks me how my day was, as if my days can be one way or another. She asks if I saw anything good on television, if I read anything good on the Internet. But there is nothing left for me to say.

"Do you need anything?" she asks. Her simple offers are the hardest to bear, like she's pressing on a bruise. She has not yet given up on me. It is her nature to care—she must care and give care and take care—and it's something I didn't fully realize about her until we had our son.

"I think about you all day," she says. She waits for a response, as if I might say *me too,* or come out and give her a hug. She says that sometimes she comes down the hallway real quiet and just sits there listening to me. There's not much to hear, but she listens anyway. "Don't think I'm trying to spy, okay? I'm not nosy, I just . . . I'm afraid that if I speak . . . it starts out so simple, just that I miss you, that I want to talk to you like I used to talk to you, maybe even hear your voice again, but then I always end up so angry. I hate when I get angry." She releases a deep breath. "And besides, I don't know if it's better to leave you alone or come and talk. Am I the problem, or can I help?"

She is sitting on the floor now. We are mere inches apart, but all we have are our voices. "Why did we get married in winter? Winter is a horrible time to get married." Today must be the day. It must already be January. Late January. The twenty-second. "I can still see a future. Can you? We could try again, we're young, it's not too late . . ."

"Won't it always be between us?" I say. "We're tainted. We'll always have this dark thing between us, dividing us. How can we be together if we're separated by this atrocious thing?"

"Or maybe it doesn't divide us. Maybe it keeps us together. Have you ever thought about that? Maybe it's glue."

Are we really bound together, forever, no matter what? What dissolves the glue, what grants freedom?

The doorbell rings. "That's our anniversary dinner," she says.

She eats alone in the kitchen. Pizza. Pepperoni, from the smell of it, and bitter onions. She uncorks a bottle of wine. The gurgle of two glasses being poured. They *ting* together, as a toast. She says something but I can't make it out.

Before I withdrew, when I lived out there, I sometimes wondered what I would do if my wife didn't come home. I wondered what would happen if—wrong place, wrong time—she got hit by a car or a stray bullet, if one day I came home from work to find only gaping silence and the reminders she left behind, her perfume, her jewelry, her ticket stub collection from so many of our dates. And her dirty laundry in the hamper, I would feel so foolish, but I couldn't just throw away her dirty clothes like read newspapers. During those wondering times I hoped that if there was a heaven or some great next life, that it wasn't the kind that could look down on Earth, so she wouldn't have to see me wandering the empty apartment like an abandoned pup. So she'd be spared my tears, my meals taken alone. So she wouldn't suffer through my sleepless nights and empty days.

And then there were the early mornings when I'd wake up before her but stay in bed and listen to her somniloquies and brush the hair from her face and I'd wonder what would happen if the stray bullet or speeding car hit her but did not kill her, but instead left her paralyzed, trapped in her body, if all she could do was blink. I wondered which of us would feel more helpless. And I wondered which of us would find it more unbearable.

"Darling," she says, "I saw someone today." The sun has set, my room black but for the streetlamps pressing against my window shade, scattered light diffused like mist. "I saw someone who I think can help us."

"Don't you mean *me*?" Me. The one with the problem.

"I mean us. We're still together, aren't we? Anyway, this woman, she . . . Thomas, this is it, my last idea for you. Your last chance. I can't stay out here forever, alone. This isn't the real you, but after this I give up. So give her a chance. Here, read this." She slides an envelope under the door.

The burning starts again, the chewing, all over my skin. The searing pain of inexpressible remorse. How long before it eats me entire?

I did not come inside one day, shut the door, and decide never to come out. I needed a day to grieve. Then a week. A month. Tired, I took a nap. When I woke it was dark. The walls were high. There was no way out.

On my dresser is a pile of framed photographs, face down. I don't need people looking at me. But sometimes I turn over a few of the photographs. That naked smiling baby in the bath, cigarette-butt penis and giant balls, and that baby on the floor, struggling to keep his head up, it's me. I wish I could've stayed that way forever. It seems

I'm caught in some giant flow, moving in one direction, but I think I've stopped it. Within these walls, I have stopped it.

The little boy standing on a shiny, wet stone pointing at the river: that's me, too. Look at my smile, at the water rushing past. I am pointing at the river but I'm looking into the camera, a peculiar expression on my face, happy but tinged with sadness, as though I grasped even then that the photograph would outlive the subject.

Four in the morning and she is out there cleaning the apartment, floor to ceiling. A bucket of water: filled, emptied, filled, emptied as the night goes on. She splashes and scrubs, she slides furniture across the floor. The vacuum cleaner sucks on the rug. Bottles spraying. Paper towels ripping. The violent snap of plastic garbage bags opening. Every month or so, maybe every three weeks, the same thing. She doesn't sleep.

I crouch over the envelope. My name is written in careful letters, a woman's writing but not Silke's. The letterforms are soft and fluid, as though the ink is barely sticking to the paper, as though my mere breath might scatter her gentle strokes. I do not open it; I leave it on the floor, my name staring up at me.

Five

THE NEXT DAY. Or week. Hard to tell. There is a pest at my door, a dispatch from my wife, a new thorn for my side. She says she's from Japan. Asks if I read her letter. Says she wants to be my sister. Says she just wants to talk, says I should open the door and let her in. Says she has a gift for me. Wants to hear my voice, to know I'm alive. Says I'd enjoy her company. Says we'd have a good time together.

But I don't need a sister. My parents said that, before me, there was a girl who would have been my sister, had she survived, but I wonder if, had she survived, they would've conceived me. They might've been too content and too happy to make another. And even if so, the same sperm would not have fertilized the same egg to yield the same me. No, I am here because my sister isn't. My parents created, lost, and created again. Whence sprang that urge to create, to add to the existence of things, to set another ball rolling? They had to try again, to again taste the godlike power.

I, too, created and lost, but I will not create again.

Go away, girl. Be someone else's sister.

But she stays at the closed door and talks. I unfocus my ears and hear only sounds, sweet sounds like a bird, all rhythm and cadence, sounds but no meaning, just up and down like notes on a page.

Fly away, bird. Be someone else's pest.

The letter still lies there, unopened on the floor where my wife slipped it in. The pest has been chirping for quite some time now. Maybe she lives inside my head, there and nowhere else. Or maybe the voice comes not from inside my head but from the envelope. I push it back under the door, ridding myself of it. The voice goes silent.

But then as I stand up, as my knee cracks, the envelope appears from the slit once again but this time it's torn open and empty, followed by a single sheet of paper, unfolded, displaying more of that same graceful handwriting. Oh, you clever thing.

Now I focus my ears and listen for what she says next. But no words come. I wait, but nothing. Only silence. An opened letter, so clever, but nothing else. So much chirping and now you're mute? Tell me more. Let me listen.

Silence. Then the clicking shut of the front door. Down the hall and through the living room, somehow without me hearing. She must have floated. Before I know it I am at the window. The shade is pulled down to the sill. I pause, then go back to my bed. I don't need to look outside to know the pest is scurrying away.

Six

As MEGUMI WALKS TO the bus stop, Silke calls from her office. "What did he say?" she asks.

"Didn't say anything, just—"

"Nothing?"

"I heard him moving around in there, but in an hour he didn't say anything."

The M10 bus approaches and Megumi quickens her pace. She rarely takes the subway. Compared to the Tokyo subway, it's slow and foul and primitive, so instead she takes the bus, which is also slow and foul and primitive but at least she can look out the windows at the people on the street, people she'll never know.

"Now what?" Silke says. "What do we do?"

"Smooth stones in a stream."

"What?"

"Smooth stones in a stream. They don't become smooth overnight."

"I see . . ."

"It's nothing to worry about. Remember, I don't stop coming."

"I just thought—"

"I know you did. But don't worry. I'll call you next time."

That night Megumi eats dinner alone in her apartment. Naoko calls and says the girls are headed out, western bars this time. She needs no convincing.

The bar is dark and humid, bodies packed tight. She and the girls are targets. She feels their stares, their desires. On her way back from the bathroom, someone grabs Megumi's ass. She stops and turns but in the crowd it's impossible to tell. Coward.

"Megumi, be careful," Miku says. "You're spilling." Beer from the wide glass is sliding down her cheek and neck. She wipes it off with the back of her hand.

They are drunk and sweaty when they stumble outside into the night, coats on but open, handbags hanging from their arms. Megumi sucks in the cold air, and goose bumps cover her skin. Miku slips on an icy patch and falls but then gets right back up and says, "Where to?"

"How about my place?" Naoko says. "I have some weed."

As Megumi lights the pipe, Naoko pours three glasses of sake. "Aren't I a great host?" she says.

"Kampai!"

Megumi settles onto the sofa. Smoke hangs in the air and crawls into her lungs and she is warm again. "To my brother!" she says, raising her glass. They all drink.

"To your brother," Miku agrees. She takes a hit, hands over the pipe, and a somber mood passes over them.

Megumi's skin is hot and red. She wants a glass of water, but she does not leave the sofa. She feels the entire circumference of her eyeballs, two stormy planets lodged into her skull. Who put them there? Time passes either quickly or slowly, she can't tell the difference.

"Hey, where are the guys?" Naoko asks.

"Who?"

"There were so many hot guys at the bar, but where are they now? Why aren't they here?"

"Looks like we forgot to bring them home," Megumi says.

"Megumi, I thought you were supposed to bring them, you're the hot one," Miku says as she swallows another glass of sake and pours three more.

"You think any of those white guys can tell us apart?" Megumi says.

Miku pours a glass of sake down Megumi's throat. She chokes as she swallows. They laugh. She lifts her feet and lies down on the sofa.

In the middle of the night she wakes to a putrid stink. She coughs as though the stink is coming from inside her, as though coughing will expel it. Naoko is sleeping on the floor, naked. Miku is curled up in a ball, still fully dressed, next to a pile of vomit.

She sits up and stretches and steps over the girls on her way out. The narrow downtown streets are empty. She presses her arms to her chest against the cold. Her head pounds with every heartbeat.

At home she spreads out her futon on the floor, covers herself with a blanket, and falls asleep. Later, she reaches in the dark for her ringing cell phone. *"Moshi moshi,"* she answers. The blended voices in the background have the unmistakable Japanese melody, and she pictures him sitting alone at a dark Shinjuku bar, in some twisted, neon-hued back alley, tie loosened after work, drinking himself into oblivion.

"It's my heart, Megumi. It beats so fast, like it might burst right out of my chest."

"Dad, what are you saying? Are you having another heart attack?" She sits upright.

"No, it's just that—"

"Do you need to go to the hospital?"

"Why won't you come back to Japan?"

She hangs up on him and pulls the blanket over her head. For a while there is silence, peace, then the phone rings again. She does not answer. Another silence, then more ringing. When it is over, she falls back asleep.

A chime wakes her, a text message from her father: I'M LONELY. She stares up at the ceiling and wonders how old the cracks in the plaster are, and how many before her have stared up at them. The cracks remind her of the spider webs in Yoyogi Park that she used to see during long Sunday walks with her father. She would hold his big hand as they walked, and he looked at the trees and birds and turtles, but she looked at the webs—wide enough to span the trees—and the spiders that had spun them, spiders as big as her head, just sitting in their webs, waiting, seeing everything but doing nothing.

She calls her father. "Get out of the bar, okay? Go home and get into bed."

"It's been long enough, you've proved your point . . . you can come back now. People forget."

"Have you eaten?" She hears him take a hard swallow of booze, then a grunt.

"We don't have to stay in Tokyo," he says. "We could move somewhere else, both of us together, a fresh start. I'm sick of the fucking office. Reporting for duty, Sir! Maybe I could start my own shop or something. Work with my hands, do something real. And you could work out front at the counter. You and me."

"Go home. And pick up a *bento* along the way." Heavy breathing into the phone, she can almost smell the alcohol. "Tell me you'll go home and eat something, okay? Dad?"

"If you were here I wouldn't be out here like this tonight. Does that make sense, do you know what I mean? Well anyway the inside of my mouth is all sticky. I'll call you later," he says and hangs up.

The day's first dull light presses stronger and stronger against her eyelids. Trying to ignore her racing thoughts only makes it worse. She finally gives up trying to fall back asleep.

She folds up her futon and places it on the shelf in the closet, then fixes herself a simple breakfast of rice, salmon, and orange wedges. The window next to her small table is always left open a crack, letting a bit of winter's bite into the apartment. Today is like yesterday, gray and steely, a uniform ceiling of clouds pressing down on the rooftops. She looks out at her apple tree, the only apple tree on Reade Street, leaves fallen, now showing off its true shape, graceful branches cutting through the air like frozen ink strokes.

She puts the dishes in the sink for later. After her shower she soaks in steaming hot water. Above the tub is a small window that she always keeps open, and through it she can see the windows of nearby buildings and she wonders if someone is spying on her as she bathes. Let them spy. The tub is the reason she took the apartment three years ago. A porcelain, claw-foot tub, deep, just like in Japan. *Ofuru.* The kind she can sit inside with hot water up to her neck, the kind she can fall asleep, slip down, and drown in.

Her father is probably not leaving. Probably still at the bar. Just one more glass. Kampai!

Megumi, he used to say, most people think the day begins when you wake up in the morning and ends when you go to bed at night. Going to bed is the last thing they do. But I make it the first thing I do. A good night's sleep ensures a good day, so I begin my day by going to bed. Tomorrow begins tonight! But he has forgotten his own advice.

She wants to keep soaking, to float all day in hot water, but she has to go visit Thomas Tessler again, who so far is just a pile of silence behind a locked door. When she leaves her building, a cat is sitting on the top step. It stands up and stretches and rubs against the iron railing. "Were you waiting for me again?" she says in Japanese. "Don't you have any warm place to stay?" The cat looks up at her, circling at her feet. "I'm sorry, sweetie, you can't stay with me and I don't have any food with me this time." The cat rubs against her leg. "Okay, wait here."

She goes upstairs, returns with a small plastic container of the dried salmon left over from breakfast, and sets it on the step. From a half block away she turns around to check but the cat is looking the opposite way, licking its paw.

The sun hasn't shone in a long time. After three years here, she isn't sure what New York is, in the larger sense. She's sure there *is* a larger sense, because in Tokyo she always had in mind both where she was at the moment and how that place related to the entire city. But in New York, she has no sense of context, no idea of what lies beyond where she is at that moment. Her New York is nothing more than what is right in front of her face. Streets, addresses, bus routes, walk or don't walk.

His locked door is waiting. She wishes she knew how to pray. The time seems right for a prayer.

Seven

THE LITTLE PEST IS back at my door. I reach into my pocket and finger her letter. I'm not sure how many days it's been since she opened it for me, since her last visit, but in that time I've read the letter 158 times after I began keeping track and at least fifty before that.

"Thomas, it's me again, Megumi." She knocks three times, gently. "Are you in there? I understand if you don't want to talk, that's okay, but at least let me know if you're in there. So that I'm not out here talking to myself."

She knocks again. I am careful not to make a sound. Someone is in here but whether that person is still me is hard to say.

"Okay, how about this," she says. "I'll stay for ten minutes, just in case you are in there, but if I don't hear from you by then I'll leave. Ten minutes is my maximum limit for talking to myself."

Her voice is an accent she's trying to hide, which makes it more noticeable. I try to imagine what she might look like, but I come up blank. People are so foreign; I can barely even remember what my own wife looks like now. I only see her in the dark, sleeping under that blanket as I pass by.

"Whatever we talk about, I'm not going to tell anyone. Not even your wife. I'm not a doctor or anything, and I'm not going to shrink your head, but even if all we talk about is your favorite breakfast cereal, it'll stay locked up inside me, okay?"

Seven minutes until she leaves. She says she took a bath this morning. Says she wanted to soak all day, but she had to come see me. Tells me to say something. Otherwise it's a wasted trip. "And I don't mean bath the way Americans mean it," she says. "I mean it the Japanese way. In Japan, first you wash, then you soak. There's a washing area, sort of like a shower, where you scrub and clean and get all soapy, and next to that is a soaking tub. You make sure to scrub everywhere, even between your toes and behind your ears. Then you rinse off and soak in the tub."

Against my will, I have an erection. Her voice. I am now mere animal. Six more minutes.

"But, do you know what's even better than a tub on a cold day like today? The *onsen*. Do you know 'onsen'? It's an outside Japanese bath. A hot spring. My parents used to take me all the time, and when I got older I went with my friends. There you are, in a huge pool of steamy mineral water, outside in the beautiful mountains, fresh air, birds and trees all around you as you soak. It's immaculately luxurious and relaxing. You've never been so clean and refreshed in your life."

Five minutes. The wind blows stronger, hissing, spitting at the window.

"Thomas, did you know there's even an onsen here? Way up by Lake Placid, up in the mountains, a Japanese family owns it. My boss Hamamoto closes the store for a week and takes us girls there every summer. She knows the owners. It's very serene and cool. Special. The place is so far from anything that you forget all about the outside world. It disappears. Just the wind and water and trees and deep-deep quiet."

My erection, mind of its own, doesn't go away. "I wonder what you look like," she says, her voice so close to the door. "Don't you wonder what I look like? It's not that I care what you look like, not like your looks matter to me, you could be anything at all and I wouldn't mind."

I try ignoring it.

"Something about the way you were before . . . you must really be worth it. Your wife doesn't want to let you go. Even I know that, just from listening to her talk about you. She's made me so curious about you . . . I like going with Hamamoto and the girls in the summertime, but it's even better in the winter. It's so beautiful to sit naked in hot sulfur water outside in the cold air. Your wet hair actually freezes into icicles, but you're so warm. An amazing sensation. If you're lucky, it snows. You and I should go sometime. Your wife can come, too. If you want."

Under the weight of my resolve, it finally shrivels away.

"Thomas, look what I made for you." She slides a piece of folded paper under the door. "It's a penguin. Because it's so cold out. You know, when romantic men want to get a girl they fold origami for her. They fold a thousand little cranes. Do you like him?"

Ten minutes have come and gone. I turn the tiny penguin over and over. She has done a nice job. I push it back under the door.

She sits in silence. She does not reprimand me, she does not beg me to come out.

"I used to sell my panties," she chirps. "My first year of high school, when my friend and I went to Shibuya for some shopping. Do you know Shibuya? Have you ever been to Tokyo? Just eye-shopping, because we had no money, but my friend said we could make some. She took me to a small building on a side street behind the convenience store. A 7-Eleven, I think."

Her voice gives her youth away. It has not yet hardened, it still carries in its melody the hope that things can be different from the way they are now, that we have the power to change the course of events.

". . . was like a doctor's waiting room. But there were no chairs, there was just a pretty girl behind a reception desk."

Silke must be paying her a lot. One hundred, two hundred a visit. Or maybe she's not paid by the visit, but rather a long-term contract. For a long-term problem. A thousand a month? Maybe a fat bonus when I come out of my room for good.

"The receptionist picked up a Polaroid camera and leaned forward. My friend lifted up her skirt."

She thinks she's going to teach me something, that she holds some key to life that is so magnificent and profound that I will abandon this little tomb and dive headfirst into the outside world.

". . . then she pulled off her panties. They got stuck on her shoe and she started falling over, so she grabbed my arm. Somehow I kept us both standing. She dropped her panties into the red box and whispered, 'Don't embarrass me.' So I lifted up my skirt, and the receptionist took the picture of my legs and panties . . ."

I doubt this is what it's like to actually have a sister. This girl is too easy, I see right through her, and it's sad my wife thought she stood a chance against me, that this chirping thing is her last idea for me. ". . . and I took off my panties and dropped them into the box." She thinks she's seducing me with this story of hers. She thinks the lonely man in his room can't resist fresh meat, that I'll open the door for it. She thinks that's all she has to offer. Flicking this pest away will be easy. Her story isn't even true.

"The pretty receptionist gave us each an envelope of money. I was afraid some pervert would look up my skirt and see that I'm not wearing anything, and my friend said, 'Some pervert's going to do a lot worse than that when he opens the box and gets ahold of your panties.'"

But if it's sad then it's also desperate, which I can't ignore.

". . . took off my panties at home at the end of the day, I got nothing, but if I took them off at the Agency, I got an envelope of money."

And yet snapping my fingers won't bring him back or reset our lives.

". . . old perverts get these packages delivered to their home or their office in a plain brown box." It seems she, too, has left behind a life, and here we both are, within feet of each other but separated by this door. ". . . sits on his desk all day, in full view of all his co-workers, and only he knows what's inside, and he's dying to open it. Probably drives him crazy, probably has a hard thing under his desk. And I always wondered what would happen if another worker in the office gets the same package, if there's an office and on every guy's desk there's this plain box and each one of them knows what's inside but nobody says anything. Imagine it. All those salarymen, all those boxes, all those panties . . ."

She is quiet for a long time. We are both quiet. The apartment itself is the only thing making any noise. The baseboard radiator pops. The cooling fan inside my DVR hums softly. Inside the wall, water sloshes through a pipe, headed to or from my neighbors, who have no idea that I hear their pipes and can guess what they're up to, that flushing and brushing and washing and showering and bathing are all distinct sloshes. My little refrigerator is normally just a faint whir, but now the thermostat clicks and the electrical circuit closes and the heat exchanger starts up with a pronounced sustained buzz. It all harmonizes into a single dull minor-key moan.

"Thomas, will you open the door for me?" Her voice has dropped. Darker. More serious, more natural. Maybe this is the real her. "I really want to meet you," she says. I stay quiet. She says we don't have to talk about *it,* that we can talk about anything, that we'd have a good time together.

She gives up. The front door shuts and the big lock snaps tight. I pull back the window shade, just a bit, but what bright sunlight! My eyes screw down to pinpricks, a stinging pain, and when it subsides, I see her, down the front steps and onto the sidewalk. The pesky little pest is a red jacket and long black hair from underneath a blue knit hat with a fuzzy ball on top. She walks away quickly.

Eight

MEGUMI FEELS CHRIS'S OR Crosby's or Kale's (she has forgotten his name) warm hand on her thigh, inching upward, inside her skirt. He stops. She knows she should give some sort of sign, but her head is spinning and when she tries to stop her head the rest of her body spins like an axle. Doing nothing is also a sign: he inches farther, a fingertip or two on her panties, brushing up and down. The music thumps. The confetti lights blink and sweep the crowd, slicing through the dark.

"Where are we?" she blurts out. He yanks his hand out of her skirt.

"What do you mean?" Naoko says. "We're right here in the—"

"I don't mean the club, I mean everything. What is this place? Why aren't we in Japan?"

"You want to go back to Japan?"

"I just mean . . . this place doesn't seem real to me, like none of the things we do here are real . . . a dream place, far from home . . . so I wonder if it's real."

"A couple too many for Megumi," Naoko says.

Megumi hops off the guy's lap and makes her way through the crowd. Naoko grabs her arm just before reaching the door. "Seriously," she says, "are you okay?"

"I'll be fine. Just need some air. I'll be back in a second."

But she does not go back. She starts walking. The streets are empty, not a taxicab in sight. The M6 bus stop is five frigid blocks away. Rats crawl over a pile of garbage bags. The garbage bags rustle. Is this place real?

She sits at the bus stop alone, bouncing her legs up and down for warmth, blowing on her hands. A man stares at her bare legs. In the quiet of the night she hears the approaching bus from a long way off.

She climbs the steps, dips her card into the fare machine, and looks for a place to sit. The odor of the bus washes over her, attacks her insides, a thick swirl of chemical cleaning solvents and lingering fast food. She tries breathing shallowly, through her mouth, but her tongue can taste the air, the hamburgers and onions and potatoes and the fat they were fried in. Won't someone open the windows?

As she steps into the aisle, the passengers—in the lifeless fluorescent light they look like stiffs in a morgue—give her strange looks, as though they hope she won't sit next to them, and in the end, despite the empty seats, she decides to stand. She holds a vertical steel pole. It feels good to grab the bus this way, to feel its vibrations, the revving and winding of the engine, as though she's taking its pulse. She looks around at the people who've been giving her strange looks and thinks, What sad people the bus brings together. Only here, only now, never again.

A teenage couple, self-absorbed, her leg draped over his, making out. From time to time he cups her breast in his hand, though she pulls it away. He must feel her gaze. He takes his lips off his girlfriend's and turns toward Megumi. If looks, as Americans say, could kill.

A middle-aged man in shabby clothes, sitting in a sideways seat, staring out the opposite window, eyes glassy, rocking slightly back and forth and moving his lips in some sort of rhythmic mumble, as though reciting a list over and over in his mind. *Juice, eggs, safety pins; juice, eggs, safety pins.* Or a prayer, one they both could pray together. *Oh please Lord end it quickly, end it soon, or at least explain how things got this way, how I ended up outliving my loved ones and drove the rest away, mercy Lord, please tell me my sins, for I'd ask forgiveness if I knew what they were.*

Does she fit among these people? She looks down on herself: high heels, knee-high socks, short skirt, open jacket. Yes, she fits in perfectly. Is this what drove Thomas into his room? Was he on a bus one day and realized he was no different from anyone else and never would be? She's seen him five times already. Hamamoto said she could leave work and go visit him whenever she needs to. More specifically, she's seen his bedroom door and nothing else. Last time, she sat outside his door for an hour telling him stories about her old life in Japan and her new life in New York. Some of the stupid things she's done, and some of the good things. She's asked about his life now and his life before. But he's been completely silent.

The bus stops and the teenagers get up to leave and as they pass the boy mutters to her. "Crazy Chink, wanna watch me fuck her?" The doors close behind them and the bus moves on.

Thomas's silence has changed. It used to tell her to stop, that he was indifferent. Now it tells her to go on; that he's soaking up her every word. A weird idea, but she can't help feeling it. Any other guy would've injected himself into her stories, argued with her interpretations, admonished her or praised her for her choices, schooled her on what she could've done better. But he lets her talk. He doesn't dispense advice or tell her what to think. What kind of person feels no need to express his thoughts? Who knows, maybe he hates her, but he accepts her. She can feel it. Nobody else would've been able to stay silent and let her be herself. Especially an American. Americans love to tell her what they think about something. But not him.

He sits and listens. Of course it could all be in her head. Silence is silence. It doesn't sound like anything. But it's also true that there are different kinds of silences, and one is the kind that draws you closer.

She gets off at her stop but she doesn't go home. She just walks. Right on Church Street. Left on Reade. She walks and walks randomly through the streets, black like coal. Everything is still, the city on pause, a heavy silence as everyone waits to resume again.

Between two buildings she catches a glimpse of the Brooklyn Bridge's tall stone towers, like a beacon. She makes her way toward the bridge, and when she reaches the foot she keeps on going, up the boardwalk. A few cars slide along beneath her, but she's the only one on the footpath. She climbs the bridge to the crest, then sits on a bench facing midtown. On television, in the movies, New York seemed so bright, gleaming, fueled by dreams. But it's not as bright as Tokyo, and not as big, and not as energetic. New York is dark and lonely and dead. The river's bluster stings her face.

The sky resolves, the sun inching closer to the horizon, and she's still on the bench. Her father calls and asks what she's doing. "I'm sitting on the Brooklyn Bridge," she says.

"It's winter—don't get yourself sick. Do you know what day it is?"

"I know."

"I loved him, you know. I never thought even one bad thing about him, ever. Do you believe me?"

"It doesn't matter."

That day she leaves her shift early and goes to see Thomas. There's always a strange gray smell in his apartment, if not the smell of death then not the smell of life either. She slips off her shoes. Poor socks, foreigners don't understand the stress taking off her shoes in their homes causes her. No matter how clean they think they keep their homes, they wear shoes inside and so a film of city muck covers their floors. In Japan, even the meanest ditch digger takes off his shoes upon entering a home. But here, she is the foreigner. She wonders if Thomas wears shoes in his room.

The apartment has a vintage feel, high tin ceilings, polished wood floors, exposed pipes and beams overhead and running down the wall, a stylish design. But everything is frozen in place like a museum exhibit, not a place for lived lives. There is a stasis to it: Silke has kept the apartment clean and tidy, like the parent of a missing child who keeps the room preserved just as it was, for the day the child returns.

There is a piano in the living room, the kind that stands up against the wall, the kind she played as a child. What if she sat down, cracked her knuckles, and began playing? There must be some songs still stuck in her fingers, even after all these years, even from childhood. Mozart, she could play Mozart. At peace in there, doing whatever it is he does, then suddenly, Mozart, badly played Mozart floating through the apartment, bouncing off the walls and floor, echoing. That would get him out of his room, if only to make her stop.

The piano keys are hidden underneath a cover of dark wood. She runs her fingers along the smooth wood but does not open it. The piano is old. The corners are scuffed and misshapen from so many slight impacts. The top is stained with circles from drinks set down as someone played. Is this a live piano that plays music, or a dead piano that plays only memories?

From the couch she picks up a blanket and throw pillow and takes them to the end of the hallway, where she assumes what's become a comfortable position: lying on her back on the blanket, knees bent, her head against the door and resting on the pillow.

She folds the excess blanket over herself. So warm. So dark. A womb. She falls asleep.

She wakes to noises from his room. Without thinking, as though still in a dream, she exclaims, "Thomas?" The noises stop. "It's just me," she says. The pillow smells faintly of a woman's perfume. She imagines Silke, her head on the pillow, flipping through the channels, waiting for a respectable hour before officially going to bed.

The sound of his mattress, then the creak of a floorboard: he moved, and sounds as though he's right next to the door. "Thomas," she says, "I'm sick of talking to the door. Go get a pen and paper. I want you to write a question on the paper and slide it under the door. You can do that, right? Just any question at all, whatever you want." She knows he won't, of course, that from his room will come only silence. She stretches her legs and opens her eyes wide and then, from under the door, a single sheet of white paper. Eight and a half by eleven. She sits upright. In the exact center of the paper, in small scribbled letters, it says *go away*. She tells him that *go away* is not a question, and slides the paper back under the door. It comes back a few seconds later. To the original he has added some extra words and a question mark, so that it now reads *Will you please go away?* She's sorry, she says, but she can't go away. Not yet. Try a real question this time, she says, and pushes the paper under the door. But it doesn't come back. Okay, she says, here's a question for you. "Do you have any brothers or sisters?"

The paper slides into the hallway. He has written the word *No.* She slides it back. "My brother," she says, "was just like you. He withdrew into his room, too." She blurts it out before she can snap her mouth shut. "Thomas, can you open up? So much easier if you open up. Don't you think? More potential for conversations or whatever else."

She paces up and down the hall. She sneaks into Silke's room. Queen bed, unmade. Open closet packed with clothes. She looks through the hanging dresses and tops, a mix of cheap and expensive, all stylish and all size four to six, all too big for her. On the shelves are stacks of folded jeans and sweaters. Underneath, on the floor, a pile of shoes and boots. She tiptoes around the bed, to the dresser. Some thin leather belts. A small jewelry chest. She opens a drawer and thumbs through Silke's earrings. Back in the hallway, the eight and a half by eleven is sitting on the wood floor, slightly askew. She reads the question.

"No," she says, "my brother's not in his room anymore. He spent four years inside but he's out now."

She slides back the paper. She hears the pen scratching against the paper, and in a moment it's back in the hallway. She reads his ragged handwriting.

"Yeah, I guess you could say I helped him out," she says, pushing back the paper. "Why won't you let me in?"

When the paper comes back, he has flipped it over, and on the new side of the sheet there is only one question. *Is your brother okay now?*

She stares at the question, wondering about the truth, and wondering what she should tell Thomas. She lies back down on the blanket. "Yes," she says, "I suppose . . . you could say he's doing better now."

He's happy?

"He's dead. Today's the anniversary."

Thomas does not respond.

"He was assaulted," she says. "Is that the right word? Maybe *fight* is better. He got into a fight. But, he didn't start the fight, and he didn't fight back."

It was the middle of the night, she tells him, and he had sneaked out of their apartment to go to Family Mart for some food. He loved ham and tomato sandwiches with cut-off crusts. The fuckers stole his sandwiches, and later the police gave her all the things they had collected from him, and the plastic shopping bag was splattered with dried brown blood. She read the receipt. She doesn't know why she read it, maybe just because he might have read it, too, before he was assaulted. The receipt showed three sandwiches. But there were no sandwiches. Beat him and sliced him and stole his sandwiches. Probably took them somewhere and washed them down with beer.

They got a call, and she and her parents rushed to the hospital. The nurse behind the desk said they had to go quickly to his room, because he was being uncooperative. Not acting in his best interest.

"A doctor and some nurses and two big men—I'm not sure what the word for them is—and the big men were tying my brother's legs and wrists to the bed. He fought them, he kicked and punched the air. Two more big men rushed in. It took four of those big men to pin him down. While he fought, his purple and bandaged and swollen face smiled at me. *Racist blood.* That's what he shouted at the top of his lungs, over and over. *Don't give me that racist Japanese blood.* He was looking at our father. But they tied him down and gave it to him. Then, suddenly, he stopped fighting. He was lying there, perfectly still. As the blood flowed into him, all the rage drained from his face, like spring snows melting away."

For him the fight was over, she says, but only she knew what that meant. She knew what he was going to do. She started crying. Her mom and dad left the room, then the big men and the doctor. It was only her and a nurse and blinking lights and plastic tubes. And a bad smell. She took a seat in the chair next to his bed, reached out, and held his hand. He closed his eyes. "His hand felt so hot in mine. Such life inside him. I told him it wasn't too late to change his mind. I begged him. I told him I didn't understand. And do you know what he said? He said, 'You only want to understand so you can stop me. But there is no stopping me. If you truly understood me, you wouldn't even try.'"

A sudden metallic sound startles her. She opens her eyes and sits upright. She stares at the knob. It seems to take forever. Finally the knob turns a quarter turn and stays there, like he won't pull but also won't let go, like his arm is absorbing the torque while he reconsiders. She stays quiet and waits. She tries not to even breathe. Then the door opens, only an inch or two, enough to see inside through a narrow strip of light. The knob unwinds. She waits for the strip of light to grow wider. Instead, she hears the floorboards squeak and the mattress springs compress.

Nine

I AM NOT LOOKING AT her, I cannot look at her, but in the corner of my eye I sense her, a slight movement toward me, just a shadow, a figure in my room, someone besides me, and my world seems to have run out of space, is barely bigger than my body, and I have nowhere to go, I am trapped here on my bed and I am not breathing. She stands still now; the shadow keeps her distance. I let out a breath and gulp down another, like I'm diving down to the bottom of the ocean. I stare just in front of my crossed legs at a spot on my bed, my eyes a powerful microscope, and I can see the tiny threads and the little creatures nesting in their weave. My gaze is searing hot. I might set the sheet ablaze.

She moves no closer but I see her head twisting around, taking in my surroundings. What have I done? I look down to see if I am wearing clothes today, for I feel naked, chills running in waves over my skin. She left the door wide open, my oxygen rushing out, leaving me with nothing, water rushing in, I float up to the ceiling and take a last gulp of air before drowning. Reduced to a pebble beneath this girl's foot. Not a plea for sympathy, merely an observation: I see how I must look to her. It's good Father and Mother aren't here to see their creation, the sum of their sweat. I hope no heaven exists from which they look down on me and regret rearing me.

Perhaps she is not here. Perhaps I am still listening to her story and my mind has raced forward to contemplate the possible effects of an as-yet-unmade decision and what I am seeing and feeling is not real but a prediction of what I would see and feel were I to open the door, and as such I am learning a lesson: that the locks belong secured and the door belongs shut.

I'm suddenly aware of an odor, wet and loamy. It's oozing out my skin, my wild hair, my clothes and sheets. I'm sure she can smell it, even from across the room, and maybe she can discriminate the urine and semen, little drops here and there marking my territory, if indeed they are present, for I can't remember what I have done and not done in here, there being until now no reason to remember, to keep track of things. It's my odor that keeps the shadow there, no closer. I have been unearthed like a cracked skeleton, evidence of some previous, now extinct existence, here this whole time just beneath your nose, waiting to be noticed.

But I am the one who opened the door. I retracted the locks and turned the knob. I am the host. She, the guest. I stare at the gaping hole. I manage to produce a syllable: "Door."

"You want it closed?"

My eyes go wide. She closes the door.

"Nice to meet you, Thomas," she says. "Thank you for letting me in."

The shadow moves closer and the image sharpens, a girl, the long black hair I remember from the window, and now a white face and small red mouth. I cannot yet see her eyes. I look away.

I lick and lick inside my mouth, massaging my palate with my tongue, but there is no saliva, no lubrication, dry on dry and all this friction, I'm afraid I'll catch fire. "Sorry," I say.

"Sorry for what?" the red mouth says.

"Brother."

"Thank you."

There is something between her and me, something in the air, particles of some sort, but the certainty with which I know the particles exist between us floating back and forth is exactly the uncertainty I have about their meaning. My odor wafting into her nostrils, she is taking me inside her.

I glance at her eyes but then look away. I do not wish to begin the interrogation. Black hair, white skin, red mouth, this is the pretty little pest my wife sent to my door. What does she expect we'll do?

Yet the interrogation has already begun: my odor, my wild hair and bristly beard, the acute angles of my limbs as I sit cross-legged on my bed, they are answers to her questions. She is taking in the sights and smells, collecting data. I am a specimen, a trapped bug. She turns and scrutinizes my room and my stacks of boxes and my clothes, judgments cementing. She thinks she already knows me.

Her head swivels. She takes another step toward me.

"Get out!" I yell, and finally my saliva is back and so I try again: "Get out!"

After she leaves I fasten the locks and rush to the window, an animal movement, an ape keeping watch, I pull aside the shade and there she is, long black hair, but this time she turns around and looks up at my window and I see her eyes and she sees my eyes, two pairs of mirrors reflecting light back and forth. She smiles at me. I snap my head back and hide behind the shade.

Every cell of every muscle is hollow, empty, and I'm surprised I don't just float away and pop like a bubble. How refreshing exhaustion is, to be completely aware of my emptiness, to feel that the slightest breeze would scatter me into oblivion. But of course there is no breeze. I will not scatter or pop; I will simply lie here exhausted from her visit.

How easily shame comes. It must have slipped through the open door, loose inside my room, and now it devours me, sharp teeth and stickywet tongue.

Ten

"WAIT THREE DAYS BEFORE seeing him again," Hamamoto says. "Now you must find the proper balance. Don't be too soft . . . don't be too hard."

But she cannot wait three days. The next morning, as soon as she is sure Silke will have left for work, she rides the M20 to the M10. Winter sadness creeps into her. The sidewalk snow piles have turned to little rocks of black ice. A thin white film covers the concrete and buildings, imparting a frozen, ashy quality, drying out like old bones. The city is a giant cemetery, buildings towering over her like gravestones, cracking apart in the cold.

She knocks on his door. The dead bolt retracts. She waits a few moments. Then she opens the door herself.

His room has a thick smell. He's again sitting cross-legged on the bed, looking at a magazine.

"Hi, Thomas," she says.

"You say my name wrong."

"I do?" she says, moving closer to him, slowly. "Will you teach me?" He does not look at her. "Can I sit here?" she asks, motioning to the bed. He moves over to create more room, and she sits facing him on the bed. "Tell me how to say it."

Suddenly he gets up and moves to the middle of the room. He sits on the floor. After a moment she does likewise. They sit opposite each other. Thomas wears an old black T-shirt. Dark blue jeans. Bare feet with very short toenails. His face is covered with dark hair, and the hair on his head is full and longish and random, clumps jutting this way and that. He looks how she imagines a painter looks, though maybe real painters don't look like what people think painters look like.

His eyes search the wood floor and finally land on Megumi's socks, colored fuchsia and blue with a little pocket for each toe. He looks at them for a long time.

"Cute, right?" she says as she wriggles her toes, ten little fuchsia balls at the end of her feet. His lips show the slightest crack of a smile, but then she blinks and it is gone. "Tell me how to say your name." She wants to reach out to touch him gently on the shoulder, a simple gesture of comfort and care and sincerity, as if to say it's okay, she's here, she's here to tear apart this world he's built, she's here to destroy it and send him back out there with his wife, back among the ills and also the beauty, but he'll be okay, because she'll be right there next to him, every step, all the way, until the end, until he's forgotten all about this little world, until he never wants to see it again. He won't be alone.

"Thomas," he says, demonstrating the proper pronunciation. "Thomas."

"Toemas?"

"No," he says. "It's German: *Toe*-mahss."

"*Toe*mass? Like that?"

"Not *aaaa* like a sheep. *Ah,* like 'open up and say *ah.*'"

"Toemahss."

"Good."

"But you aren't German, are you? Why pronounce it that way?"

"Why do you think?"

"Why do I *think*?"

"No, not 'why do you think?' Why do you think I pronounce it that way?"

"Because you told me you pronounce it that way. You just showed me. You said I got it right."

His jaw clenches. His fingers curl tightly. "I mean," he says, "can you guess why I pronounce it that way?"

She is embarrassed. Sometimes the simplest English phrases trip her up. She can go on and on about complicated thoughts and subjects, but then someone will ask her what the date is and she'll start describing how it tastes so good so many ways but her favorite is simply dried, as a snack, but you have to be careful how many you eat because, well, you know, you might need the bathroom.

She can't guess why he pronounces his name that way. She shakes her head.

"Because my father pronounced it that way when I did something good."

She has never met a foreigner who could pronounce her name correctly. When foreigners say her name she doesn't feel they're talking to the real her but some shapeless approximation.

"Want to learn my name?" she asks.

"Megumi," he says.

"Close. But try to not make an accent. Make each syllable the same. Not: Me-*gu*-mi. Me-gu-mi."

"Megumi."

"Better!" She smiles. "Now, make each syllable shorter. Don't hold the vowels so long. Not: *Megooooomiiiiii*. Make it faster. Make it more . . ." She searches for the word from childhood piano lessons. ". . . staccato. Make it more staccato. *Dit-dit-dit*. Fast. Megumi."

"Megumi."

"Yes. Yes! Now keep it stuck in your head."

"Megumi," he says.

"Thomas," she says.

Finally he looks into her eyes, but only for a moment. Then he looks away. He has such large eyes, dark and deep and sad.

Silence. The space is cluttered with stacks of boxes, tall piles of magazines, crowded shelves, a desk messy with papers and magazines and a laptop computer, a garbage bag filled with empty boxes and wrappers, but it's not a filthy room. There's a certain order to it.

The thick smell, on closer inhalation, is a humid mix of lingering food, like chemicals heated in the microwave, and of secreted human oils and dead skin cells, the smell of a person living a still life. There is also a faint bitter smell, like burnt coffee. She notices a mug next to the television and a can of instant.

He stares at the floor, his body stiff, muscles coiled so tight he's almost shaking or shivering. Just like her brother. She had no idea what memories her brother was chasing away, fighting off with those coiled muscles, and she always expected him to snap, go crazy, maybe even pounce on her. But then she'd take a slow step toward him and place her hand on his head and he'd begin to weep and his muscles would slacken and his entire body would melt into a puddle on the floor.

"You want me to come out," Thomas says.

She's supposed to say yes, that life is out there not in here, that he can't stay in here forever, that the future isn't so bad. "Life is out there, not . . ."

But—she's not sure why—she cannot continue. Silence overtakes her.

"There's no use for you here," he says. "You can't help me, and I don't want to leave."

"But if you don't think I can help, why did you let me in your room?"

He crosses his arms over his chest. "My wife asked me to talk to you. And now I have. I've let you in, and now you can report back to her how hopeless it is and we can all go back to the way things were."

She scoots a little closer. He holds his ground. The space between their knees is now just a sliver. "You've talked, but you haven't said anything."

"What would satisfy you?"

"I don't know. I've never done this before."

"This isn't your job?"

"This is the last thing I ever wanted to do."

He suddenly looks up at her.

"I'm sorry," she says. "But I'll always be honest with you. At first I didn't want to come. Your wife forced you, my boss forced me."

His gaze holds her eyes. It does not waver. His eyes hide his thoughts. They take in, they collect, but they do not let out. A one-way valve.

"You think I'm a waste of time," he says. "You think I should just die."

"Why would you say that?"

"Like your brother. You said he's better now because he's dead."

The stacks of corrugated boxes tower over them. The little refrigerator hums. A garbage truck rumbles down the road.

"I don't want you to die."

"But you don't want to be here. You don't want to see me."

"It's complicated." She learned the phrase from a movie and has been waiting to finally use it.

"Who's your boss? What's your job?"

"I'm a clerk at a wagashi shop."

"What's wagashi?"

"I'll bring you some. Next time."

"Why don't you want to help me?"

"I never said that. Why don't you want my help?"

"Because I'm fine."

"Oh yeah?"

He lets out an incipient sound that dies before it can mature into a laugh. She resists reaching out and touching his knee.

"So then let's forget about helping," she says. "You're fine, I'm fine. I'm not sure what to do, anyway. Forces have brought us together."

"What kind of forces?"

"I don't know. I feel I'm always being forced. I never get to decide. Does my English make sense to you?"

"It's very good."

"Americans expect everybody to speak English."

It's an awkward exchange, a mistimed, uncomfortable dance, neither of them knowing what to make of the other, what to say, how to proceed, but there is also a murmur of attraction—or maybe only intrigue—that keeps her searching for the thread, the spark that will get the words flowing smoothly. He is afraid of her, but already she can see that his heart harbors no hate. There was a time in her life when she was constantly with different men, strangers, sizing them up, and she learned to trust her gut, a sometimes painful education, but it paid off, and now when she looks at Thomas she feels something she can't quite put into words because it's just an instinct, but already she can see why Silke has waited and why she wants him back.

For a long time they say nothing. They both succumb to their preoccupations.

"I didn't realize there was anyone else like me," he says.

"Hikikomori? I think in this country you might be the only one. But there are lots in Japan. It's not exactly the same, but close enough."

"What happened to your brother?"

"That's why I didn't want to come. I miss him too much."

His eyes apologize but his lips stay mute. He flinches. "You're wasting your time."

"You're hopeless?"

"You can't fix me."

"I don't want to fix you."

He tilts his head like a wondering puppy. She feels as if she's talking to her brother, saying what she never had the chance to say. "I'm curious about you," she says. "But I don't want to fix you. I just want you to come back to the world."

"The more you know me, the less you'll like me. You may think you know about my son, but—"

"I didn't know you have a son."

"She didn't tell you?"

"I told her not to tell me anything. It's just me and you." The wind whistles. Then it fades.

"Tell me something about your brother."

The light through the window shade has turned dull and gray, flat and weak. "My brother wanted to be an astronomer. He had a telescope pointed out the window. He had maps of the stars. He read books about space dust. But have you ever been to Tokyo? It's too bright to see many stars. Brighter than New York. He told me all about the big bang. He told me that in the big bang energy became . . . became . . ."

"Matter?"

"Yes. In English. Thank you. He told me energy became matter."

His T-shirt is clean. No stains. The sleeves and neck have not stretched from too much time away from the washing machine. She wonders how he does laundry. Her brother washed it in the sink and hung it from a line stretching across his room. His skin, too, looks clean. He showers. He keeps up with basic human grooming. She can report back to Silke. It's enough for a seed of hope. And if he showered and dressed just for her, even better.

"Did you really sell your underwear?"

"Yes," she says. She wants his trust. She wants him to believe. "But I didn't tell you the real reason. It started out as shopping money. But then I got an idea. A stupid idea. I thought if I sold enough I could save enough to take my brother out of his room, to some other country. Somewhere dark. Where he could see the stars."

The room is too small. She goes to the window. She pulls back the shade. One corner of the glass is white with frost. "Thomas," she says, careful to pronounce it correctly, "it's snowing. Come look." He joins her at the window. He is tall. She comes up only to his shoulders.

The snow falls gently. The wind forms the flakes into translucent sheets, thin curtains swaying back and forth.

"Isn't it beautiful?" she says. Thomas watches the snow but says nothing. Megumi, too, says nothing for a time, the two of them together at the window, watching. "Snow is gentle, but so powerful," she whispers. "Slows everyone down . . . makes everything quiet."

Snow sticks to the branches of the tree to eerie effect, as though the tree is white and the branches mere shadow. Unseen birds chirp.

"What could those birds be singing about in the snow?" she says. Thomas turns toward her, on the verge, lips parted. But he says nothing.

"I know it's hard to let me in," she says, looking out the window at the white world. "I'm an invasion of privacy. My own brother hardly ever let me in. You're brave to let me in. And I can see that there's something heavy inside you."

That heavy thing, whatever it is, has gravity. It's drawing her in, closer. She feels the pull. She has been alone for so long, surrounded by people who are empty inside. It's what she thought she wanted, to float, untethered, to forget. But heavy things—even buried deep—tend to find each other. Silence attracts silence.

She touches his back. Three fingertips. He does not flinch. Now all five. She holds the pressure. They watch the snow fall. The wind picks up and the sheets of snow disintegrate into random white swirls. "Want to go outside," she asks, "play in the snow? Nobody's there. It'd be just us."

"It's time for you to leave."

"But the snow," she says. "Why don't you come out with me for just a few minutes?"

"I wish I could."

He closes the door behind her and locks the dead bolt with such deliberate slowness that it sounds as though he's trying to be quiet and gentle, as though he feels some sort of complicated emotion about locking her out, or about her hearing him lock her out. Megumi waits, not sure exactly what she's expecting, but whatever it is it doesn't come.

She peeks into Silke's room on her way out. Bed still unmade, underwear and a bra on the floor, and a pair of twisted jeans. Curtains open.

Outside she makes a snowball and hurls it at his window. It's pretty high and she misses, hitting the bricks just below. This time she packs the snow tighter and throws it harder. The snowball explodes and the window rattles and all that remains is a little white dot of snow stuck to the glass. She packs another one. She waits, and as soon as she sees the slightest movement in the window shade—there it is—she lets it fly and it arcs through the air and just as Thomas's full head appears in the window the snowball smacks against the glass. He recoils, disappears, and then there is only the window shade and two white dots. She makes another and waits, melting snow seeping into her mittens, staring up at the window, smiling.

"You know that guy?"

She whirls around and faces a man with a bright orange metal snowshovel. "Who are you?" he says.

"I'm sorry," she says, deploying her thickest Japanese accent. She turns to walk away.

"No, wait," he says. "That guy up there—how do you know

him?" He cannot hide his confusion. He looks back up at the window, then at her again, the Japanese girl throwing snowballs. He's about Thomas's age, maybe a little older, all bundled up and ready to shovel the snow.

"I'm sorry," she repeats, and turns and hurries away. When she gets to the bus stop, the snowball is just a little ball of ice. She throws it at a stop sign.

Eleven

I SCREAM MYSELF AWAKE, AND if my scream has also awakened Silke, she does not come down the hall to ask about my nightmare. She stays in her bed, busy with nightmares of her own.

In my head, the lingering echoes of a singing cardinal. The morning my son died the cardinal sang for only a minute or two, but in my nightmare she sings forever, on and on, never tiring, never a pause, an endless repeat of whoops and chirps, a rhythm and melody with no resolution, and I have no power to move forward or back; I am forced to sit and watch and listen until my mind can take no more, until an invisible biological process squirts chemicals through my blood, waking me up alone in my bed, nobody to comfort me when I scream.

The night is at its blackest. The wind wails against the window, trying to slither in. Even the wind needs refuge and relief from the cold.

I feel my way to the window and raise the shade. Snow, stained orange from the sodium lamps, covers the street. The plows have not yet come. Everything looks soft and peaceful. But the wind still blows.

I turn away from the snow and he is standing in the middle of my room, looking up at me. He is mostly shadow, but his little form is unmistakable. A father knows. His cheek, his nose, his eyes, they collect and reflect the scant light. "Why are you so scared?" he says.

"You snuck up on me. I didn't know you were there."

"Dad, what happened to me?"

"You don't remember?"

"I try, but I can't."

"I don't know either."

"Dad, why didn't you save me?"

"I didn't see it in time," I say, and I can't tell whether he believes me. This is our stalemate.

"Who is that girl?" he asks.

"What girl?"

"The one with the strange eyes."

"You saw her?"

"Are you going to marry her instead of Mommy?"

"That's not how it works."

"Because Mommy's still here."

"You talk to Mommy, too?"

"She won't talk to me. I did something wrong."

"You didn't do anything wrong. I did."

I blink and he is gone. It's always like that. I blink or avert my eyes in shame just for an instant and he's gone, from shadow to less than shadow, and some romantic place inside me wants to say that he's not actually gone, that he's still in my room, somewhere, that he's always here in my room with me. But I know it's not true. He is gone. His absence is like someone punctured my chest and vacuumed out all my organs. I find my way back under the covers, pillow still wet with nightmare sweat, I concentrate on the sound of my breathing, I hope to god the nightmare won't pick up where it left off, and I fall asleep.

"I'm proud of you—" Silke says one evening from the hallway, interrupting my magazine article about the proper way to make a schnitzel, specifically (for the sake of illustration) Wiener schnitzel, but the same techniques can be and should be and must be applied to the entire schnitzel family.

"—for letting her inside your room and letting her help." The first key is that the schnitzel must be pounded thin, thinner than you think, a point which I thought was obvious but apparently out there in the world there are a lot of thick schnitzels, some almost as thick as a proper Japanese *tonkatsu*. In a sidebar the article points out that in America a lot of tonkatsu are way too thin (but thicker than a proper schnitzel), thereby creating an entire species of breaded fried meat that is the same thickness, both of which are incorrect. I wonder if my little pest eats tonkatsu. I've never had it.

"I know it must be difficult, but . . ."

The second key is that the frying fat should be a mixture of oil and butter, and the oil should have a high enough flashpoint that it won't catch fire. The exact proportions are of course not scientifically certifiable, based instead on the experience of the cook, who must pay close attention to the cooking of thousands of schnitzels in order to stockpile a great mass of information that he synthesizes into something called intuition.

"What do you two talk about? Do you like her?"

"I'm sure she tells you everything," I say. The third key—the most important—is the level of heat involved, which must be high enough to blister the breading, but not so high it burns, and of course the ability to accomplish this is helped greatly by the proper adherence to point number two, the proper proportion and types of butter and oil.

"She doesn't tell me anything," she says.

The blisters, or bubbles, create air pockets between the breading and the meat, and these air pockets give the schnitzel its lightness. The breading should not stick to the meat, except here and there and barely, just enough for it to hold together. The article says that if your experience of a schnitzel is a leaden, oily, soggy mess of thick meat, then your cook either failed to create the air pockets or, more likely, never learned how to really cook a schnitzel in the first place.

"All she said was that you let her inside. And that you are very handsome and that you were very nice to her." Her voice overflows with pride.

Handsome? "I told her to stop coming," I say.

"Well then it's a good thing she's not going to listen to you."

"I told her it's no use."

"But it is, and you know it."

"I told her about him."

She is trying to create a home where none exists, and suddenly I feel immense empathy toward her and her life out there. To her, my presence here at the end of the hallway must be an all-consuming emptiness. For me there is only the present, but for her time continues without mercy, and sometimes I am everywhere and sometimes I am nowhere. With these feelings the world is seeping in drop by drop.

"So I was thinking," she says, "that I could cook dinner for you. If you want. Don't make a big deal of it—it's just dinner. Just dinner, then you can go back inside." Not tonight, she says, she doesn't mean she's going to cook tonight. She doesn't have any groceries tonight anyway. So she'll cook dinner tomorrow. Is it a date? she asks. But I do not respond. What do you want, she asks, she'll cook anything. Just say the word, make a request, anything at all. If it's complicated, she says, she'll call in sick from work and stay home all day cooking. So, what'll it be?

What'll it be, as if she's working the counter at a diner, pen behind her ear. "Thomas!" she shouts with a flash of fire. But then she extinguishes it and calmly continues, "Will you have dinner with me tomorrow?" There is fight in her voice, beneath the calm, a fight against me, of course, but also a fight within herself, a fight to hold back the hope, or to hold back something else.

"I'll think about it," I say.

———————————

HE WOKE UP EARLY one summer morning, and sneaked into our room and poked my shoulder and whispered close to my ear so as not to wake his mother. "Dad," he said, "how much longer? When can we go?"

"Not until later, in the afternoon," I said, rolling over, my face so close to his I could smell his milky skin. To that little creature I must have smelled ancient, unearthed, clumps of dirt sticking to my skin. "Let me sleep just a little longer," I said.

"Do you think I'll catch a ball?"

His first baseball game, his only. A cool night, barely a breeze. His first baseball hat, too big for his little head, his first bag of salted peanuts. *Dad, are you sure it's okay to just throw the shells on the ground?*

A perfect night. The green field and bright lights, the cheering, he sat with his jaw constantly dropped. *The hugest thing I ever saw.* He kept swiveling around in his seat, taking it all in. The people seated around us showered us with smiles. I cracked open the peanuts for him. He picked them out of the shell.

I wonder what it's like at the onsen. I wonder if it's as peaceful and pure as she says, I wonder if there I could wash my guilt away, wash my fear away.

My son is buried not far from here. I have never been to see him, but I wonder: if he visits me here, then has he left his grave? Did I not bury him deep enough? Has he pushed himself up through the soil?

Twelve

MEGUMI GOES TO A bar, alone. She buys a glass of vodka and sips it. Ice cubes melt against her lips. She looks closely at each man in the bar.

Some are too young. Most are too old. Most are too fat. None have beards the way Thomas has, so she imagines what he might look like under the beard. She tries to find a match. He doesn't have to be perfect. He has to be close enough. The hair is important. It has to be longish and dark and a bit ragged. The build is important. He has to be tall. But not too skinny. The eyes are important. They have to be nearly black. If he has a far-off stare, even better. Clothes aren't important. He won't need them.

It takes a while. She buys another drink. She deflects the attention she gets from men who don't match. She keeps searching the crowd.

She tells herself that this will help her keep her cool next time. The problem is comfort. She feels comfortable with him. She tells him things she shouldn't. Comfort leads to closeness. Closeness leads to desire. Desire grows uncontrollable. The heavy thing.

Just when she's about to give up, she spots him. Any hesitation might dissolve her will. She approaches him. His hair is right, and his beard, too. Next to him at the bar she pretends to be frustrated at the bartender's inattention. She leans forward to make sure he can see down her shirt, to see she isn't wearing a bra. Men are as predictable as the sun.

He orders a vodka for her. "It's on me," he says. He tells her his name but she promptly and permanently forgets it. He's nervous. Maybe his first Asian. He drones on about how the drink he's drinking is the same drink he had on his recent trip to some island's all-inclusive resort, where he got sunburn and drank so much that an entire day is still unaccounted for. So impressive! He carefully neglects to mention who accompanied him on this trip. The way he tells the story it appears he went all by himself, that he sat alone on the beach and drank himself into oblivion. So then, probably a girl-friend, perhaps a wife.

He continues. Her mind wanders to Thomas in his room. What is he doing now? Sitting down to a magazine on his bed? What she wouldn't give to be talking to him right now instead. Such a waste, this empty vessel out here in the world while Thomas, who could have a full, interesting life, sits idle in his empty room.

His place is a high-rise apartment meant to impress. She plays along as he makes her another drink and takes her to the windows to point out the *sweeping* views of the *magnificent twinkling* city. But her heart is not moved. Her heart is far away.

They sit on his sleek modern sofa. He talks about the objects in the room, where he bought them and how much they were. He is in turn boasting about how much or how little each object cost, as though at that moment she might find his skill at spotting a good value irresistibly attractive. She listens patiently, long enough to leave no question about her politeness; then she cuts him off.

"Here's how this is going to work," she says as she sets down her drink. "I'm going to direct you. I'm going to tell you everything you need to do, everything I like, how to do it and when to do it. You're not to do anything unless I say. Got it?"

"Like Simon Says."

"Simon Says?"

"It's a kid's game. Simon says, take off your pants. Like that."

"There's a kid's game that makes you take off your pants?"

"No, no, but that's how—"

"No, it's not like that. I won't be saying Simon says. I'll just be telling you what to do. Can you handle that? Can you handle me giving all the orders?"

"I think so."

"You think so?"

"Yes. I can handle it."

"That's better. Good answer. If you follow my instructions exactly, I promise you'll have a good time. If you don't follow them exactly, I promise I'll leave immediately. No second chances."

"Got it."

"Good. Now, the first thing—I'll be calling you by a different name. The whole time I'll be imagining that you are someone else. It's important you get it right. Can you handle it? Still want to go on?"

"Yes."

"Second thing—don't talk. Ever. Not one word. Your voice will ruin it. Okay, let's start. Take that magazine and go into your room and close the door. Then sit cross-legged on your bed and put the magazine in front of you and read it and wait for me to come in."

She gives him some time, so that he'll be missing her, waiting for her, wondering if she'll actually come in or if he's being played. She needs him to be anxious. She goes to the window and looks out at the city. She tries to find Thomas's street, 109th Street, but she can't separate it from the rest. When she thinks he's anxious enough, she opens the door and finds him cross-legged on the bed, looking at a magazine by the light of a single bedside lamp. She turns it off.

When it is over, when she is satisfied, she leaves his stiff embrace and his bed and takes a shower. A soak, that's what she really wants, a long, hot soak, but that will have to wait until she gets home to her claw-foot tub.

She walks naked back to his room. He is passed out under the sheet, snoring. Drunk, maybe, but mostly spent and exhausted: she made him work. She picks out her clothes from the scattered piles. She pokes him on his shoulder.

"Wake up. Time for me to go."

She pokes him again and he stirs to life, grunting a little before he speaks. "I had the doorman call you a taxi. It should be waiting." This is what passes for being a gentleman.

"Aren't you forgetting something?" she says.

"What."

"How will I pay the driver?"

"Oh. Where're my pants?"

She finds them on the floor. He fishes out his wallet and hands her a twenty-dollar bill. His gentlemanly limit.

"But," she says, "I live farther away than that."

Another twenty.

"And I'm hungry."

Another twenty.

"You're a strange girl."

"You don't even know the half of it."

"Can I have your number?" He struggles to raise his head off the pillow. One eye is completely closed, the other only a slit. He could be talking to anyone.

"No," she says, "but you can give me yours. I may need to use you again sometime."

Thirteen

MEGUMI KNOCKS ON HIS bedroom door but he does not answer. "Not going to let me in today? Are you angry with me? Tell me so I can say I'm sorry." She knocks again. She's still a little winded from climbing the stairs too quickly. Her own apartment is on the third floor and she's never winded there, but Thomas's two extra floors seem to make a huge difference.

She puts her ear to the door. "Thomas?" She tries the knob. It turns. Very gently she pushes on the door, just a test, but the bolt is not extended and the door opens. After an inch or two, she calls his name again through the crack, and again there's only silence. She opens the door the rest of the way.

Thomas is not there. Not in his bathroom either. She looks around quickly for clues, but apart from his absence, the room is exactly how it was before. Her heart jumps. She kneads her hands together. For half an hour she waits in his room, looking out the window to see if he's coming back. She finds a notebook on his desk and pulls out a sheet of paper and folds another origami penguin, just like the one he pushed back under the door. She does a better job with this one, and she stands the penguin on the windowsill, facing out, keeping watch.

She bundles up and heads downstairs. The man is there again, standing on the sidewalk, this time without a shovel. She turns the other way but he catches up to her. "How do you know him?" he asks. "I'm curious, because we used to be such good friends. And his wife, too. We used to be close."

Megumi looks straight ahead, her pace steady. "I'm just a friend," she says.

"I see. So we have something in common. We're both his friend."

"I guess so."

"But you're prettier than me—he probably likes you better. Anyway, my name's Morris."

At the corner she waits for Morris to commit to a direction, and she says she's going the other way. He tells her that he's very concerned about Thomas, and if there's anything he can do to help, she shouldn't hesitate. He lives in the next-door building, in apartment 1F. He stops following her.

She searches for Thomas block by block, looking for the odd man out. The air is crisp and fragile, the sky cloudless blue. Long winter shadows slash the pavement. She checks out all the convenience stores and even all the bars, sad places at that time of the afternoon, dark and wet and stale.

Two hours she searches for him in the raw air, sometimes on the move, up and down the blocks, sometimes standing at an intersection as she scans each passing face. Finally she decides he probably just stepped out on an errand and that he's probably already back inside his warm room, while she is outside turning into an ice cube. She goes back.

His room is still empty. The penguin still stares out the window.

Best now to wait and warm up. She goes to the entryway and retrieves her shoes. No need to spook him when he returns. She closes herself in his room, but she does not lock the door.

So this is his world. A strange excitement flows through her. She wonders if she would have the courage to sit in a room for years with only her thoughts, to ignore the possibilities and potential of a life out there and be simply content with what she found within these four walls.

His room is cleaner than her brother's was—and there's plenty of empty floor space. Her brother's only open space was a tiny hole of wood floor in front of the computer, which was also on the floor, just enough space to sit and stare at the screen all day. He spent the last years of his life on that tiny circle of floor.

What does he do in here all day? He only reads magazines, that's it? There is a computer, but it's not on, and now that she thinks about it, she's never seen it on. It's shocking for her to think that his days might genuinely be empty, that he truly has no more use for the world.

She decides that it wouldn't hurt anything to peek inside one of the boxes. There are five stacks. She picks the closest and pulls on the top box, surprisingly heavy, and it drops to the floor, her tiny muscles barely averting a complete crash.

Thousands of photographs, haphazard and loose, as though they were just thrown into the box in a hurry. She fingers through them. They are strange. Photo after photo of the same thing: toothbrushes, or actually extreme close-ups of the same toothbrush, over and over, obsessive work, each bristle rendered in intimate detail. From a little deeper in the box she pulls out large contact sheets, each with a dozen images of the same toothbrush, the red plastic handle looking like candy. Then, an entire sheet of sunglasses, different styles and colors. Another sheet of ballpoint pens, and two sheets of refrigerator magnets shaped like sunflowers. She pulls down the next box on the stack, anticipating the weight this time but still barely keeping it from crashing. More prints and contact sheets, and also a binder of large negatives, and scattered, crumpled paperwork: memos, instructions, invoices. The pictures are all similar, close-ups of products in garish detail. Stuffed animals with fur that through lighting and photo technique seem alive, three-dimensional. A whole stack of sheets with pictures of modern lamps, skeletal designs with bold colors, arms swung this way and that and in different poses, row after row of photographs. Desk lamps, floor lamps, hanging lamps, an entire lamp family showing off before the camera.

So this was Thomas's former life. Days spent photographing objects. She imagines him setting up the lights and positioning the camera and the products. Or maybe he had an assistant. Maybe his assistant was young and pretty.

The third box isn't so high, so she opens it without pulling it down. She expects to find something different, but it's more pictures of products, things to consume. She rummages all the way to the bottom but finds not even a single photograph of a human being. After a struggle the stack of boxes is back to how it was. Sweat beads on her forehead. There is a cooking magazine on the bed. She lies down and reads the open page, something about schnitzels, which apparently is a sort of breaded meat, and his bed is warm and all the searching and heavy boxes have worn her out and her mind races—where could he be?—and she falls asleep.

A slamming door. The room is black, the sun has set. She suddenly finds herself on the floor crouched behind the bedroom door. She hasn't thought about this part, about what she would do when she finally hears his footsteps coming down the hall. Maybe she should've left her shoes in the entryway as a signal that she was here, in his room. Now he's going to feel ambushed. She wants to flee, but there's nowhere to go.

Footsteps cross the living room floor and start down the hall. They stop. Then, barely audible, some sort of muffled rustling. What's he doing?

Again the footsteps but this time headed away from her. Then the sudden sound of splashing urine in the toilet. It's Silke, not Thomas. Is there a keyhole, or something Thomas has rigged to allow him to peer into the apartment? She can't find it. The door is solid and she's left to only her ears.

The toilet flushes and she strains to hear footsteps behind the sound of the swirling, cavitating water. The toilet noises fade away. The thud of pots striking each other as one is pulled out of the cupboard. The dull splashing of water filling a pot.

She sits in the dark, cross-legged on the floor. Now that she is inside she can't get out, trapped, again staring at the door but from the opposite side. Silke is chopping, knife against cutting board in regular rhythm. All this, just for herself. Maybe she enjoys cooking. Or maybe the longer it takes to make dinner, the less empty time she has to fill before going to bed.

There's something wrong about listening to this lonely woman make dinner. Something wrong, and something exhilarating. Making love to her could hardly be more intimate than this.

She used to watch her first boyfriend. He worked in a sneaker store just off Takashita Dori, a tiny place you either somehow already knew about or happened to stumble upon. The store had no sign, no windows, and through the tinted glass door you couldn't see the expensive, one-of-a-kind sneakers. All indications of the store's purpose were hidden from view. But she discovered one day as she went to meet her boyfriend that through the glass door, from across the street, at a certain angle, she could see the counter and the register and him. She stopped her approach and watched him through the passing pedestrians. So, she thought, this is how he really is when I'm not around. For a long time she stood there soaked in adrenaline, camouflaged by pedestrians, watching him. She sent him a text message just to see his face as he read it. He was doing nothing more than the simplest tasks, helping customers, ringing up sales, checking his phone, chatting with the other clerk, and she was across the street among thousands of people, yet somehow she had never felt such an intimate connection with him. She was peering into the real him.

Silke's footsteps down the hall. She knocks, gently. "Sweetie, have you thought about dinner? I'm making your favorite pork chops."

Megumi stays silent.

"Are you sure you don't want to come out, just this once?"

Her footsteps back down the hall to the kitchen. Megumi lets out a long breath, just now realizing she has been holding it. Is it over or has it only begun? Yet the thrill of it: of being inside like him, of having his life, experiencing it.

Silke keeps cooking, more chopping, urgent now, the regular rhythm has fractured. Pots and pans, running water. The sizzle of meat, the smell of meat, the salty fragrance. Plates, utensils, setting places for dinner.

Footsteps. "Are you sure you don't want to come out? I got them cut extra thick just for you. We need to celebrate. Thomas?"

Like Thomas, like her brother, she is silent.

"You know," she says from only inches away, "it's such a shame all you have is that little microwave and can't even have a decent meal. You there in that little room, just microwaving frozen dinners, me out here with all this space and the nice kitchen and fresh groceries and nice wine . . . you know, that stuff will kill you. All the preservatives in those microwave dinners, all the chemicals, they'll kill you. And when was the last time you ate a fresh vegetable or fruit? How would I know, maybe you do, right? Well, even if you do it doesn't matter much because of all the frozen shit you eat. I bet when you die your body won't even decompose. They'll bury you—I'll bury you—and your body will just lie there in the dirt, as it is, so full of preservatives. Maybe in a thousand years someone will dig up your body so perfectly preserved and they'll put you in a museum and maybe then you'll be important. What kind of life are you living in there? Is it so much better than being out here with me? Do you like those fucking microwave dinners so much? You know, I can smell them sometimes. When I come home from work, I can smell the stink coming from your room. Fucking disgusting. Makes me want to puke. You in there, me out here, it's ridiculous. How much longer can I take it? I'm making dinner for you, your favorite, why won't you come out and eat it?"

Megumi watches the two shadows of Silke's feet in the slit beneath the door. They are perfectly still.

"No, nothing? Just going to sit in there and not make a sound and ignore your fucking wife? I don't deserve a response? Just going to hide in there and scrounge around outside for food in the middle of the night, like a rat? That's the life you want?"

They share a long silence.

"Just this once?" she asks, her voice trembling. "Then you can go back inside. Jesus Christ, I'm not asking you to spend the night with me, just dinner."

Back to the kitchen. A chair pulling out, then scooting back in. Knife against plate.

"Oh sweetie!" she says from the kitchen, loudly, and as though she is talking to Thomas at the table. "I'm so glad you changed your mind. I already set a place for you and our son—we're all together again. There, sit down. Did you have a good day? Oh, don't want to talk about it? That's okay, why do couples always have to talk about work anyway? What do you think of dinner? Oh really? Even better than normal? I outdid myself this time? Thank you sweetie, it's so kind of you to say that. I'm sorry about what I said before, about you not decomposing. I didn't mean it. I'm sure you'll decompose just like the rest of us. I just get a little frustrated at times, you know? I'm sure you can understand. It gets so lonely out here without you. But now you're here, eating with me! Thank you! Thanks for tonight. Thanks for doing me the honor. I know it's hard for you. And I really concentrated on getting these pork chops just right just for you. Oh my gosh, you're wolfing them down! Be careful. Savor. Want another? No? How about one more, just one? When's the next time you'll be able to have them? Might as well get your fill now while you still can. Good, there, have another. How's it going with your rental sister? Have you made any progress? Have you fucked her yet? Sweetie, don't look at me like that. It's a legitimate question. Have you? Is she a good fuck? Does she suck your dick better than me? I bet you're staying in there just so she can keep coming. And I'm the one paying for it. No, no, that's ridiculous, isn't it. Ridiculous. She's a *sister*. I'm sorry, Thomas, sorry to have said that. And about not decomposing, sorry about that too. But I get frustrated and I say the wrong things. Can you forgive me? Eat your pork chop. I just get frustrated, you know?"

The night crawls on. Megumi sits on Thomas's bed and waits. The worst part is the helplessness. After a while, thinking about where he might be or what might have happened to him becomes useless and frustrating—it's all just uneducated guesswork—and her thoughts sink deeper. Back in Japan when her brother was in his room it felt like she and her parents were constantly waiting for him to come out and that he knew they were always ready to welcome him with open arms. That was the assumption. That the family was his safety net and when the time was right he would come out of his room to them. In other words he was the one keeping himself in his room, and the family was what would eventually catalyze his return. But now she's not so sure. Sitting here in Thomas's room, it all seems so much more complicated than that. She wonders whether at a certain point it all reverses, like how every so often the Earth's magnetic poles switch, and the loved ones waiting outside go from being a harbor to being a barrier. For her brother the thought of coming out to face her and their parents must've been paralyzing. And right now she can't leave Thomas's room because Silke is there. It might be the same for Thomas. If Silke weren't here, would he still be living in his room? Maybe the closeness that she and her parents and Silke constantly provided and provide isn't reassuring at all. Maybe it's stifling. Suffocating.

Suddenly she hears—as though it has been going on for some time but she's just now realizing it—moans, gentle at first but then more intense. Two voices, two moans, man and woman. "You like it like that?" The voice is not Thomas's. Is Silke so bold, so wicked to do it right in front of Thomas, taunting him to come out and do something about it? She wants to rush out there and—and what? Politely explain how distasteful it is to sleep with another man in front of your husband?

"Just like that just like that just like that . . ." But the voice is not Silke's. Abruptly, it stops. Footsteps to the bathroom, a few seconds of running water, then footsteps back to the living room. She's brushing her teeth. Then the sex sounds return. The television. She's watching while she brushes. Behind the groans and slapping skin she again hears the running water, and spitting.

Silke doesn't wait for the on-screen couple to finish. She turns off the television. The house goes quiet.

For a while Megumi hears nothing, then the sound of mattress springs compressing. Does Silke always sleep with the door open?

More moans, loud moans, only Silke's voice this time, from her lonely bed. She calls out Thomas's name as she does it. "Deeper," she says. "Is that all you've got?"

Megumi tries not to listen.

Fourteen

AT SUNRISE I AWAKEN but next to me the pretty little pest still sleeps. Scant space between us, I can smell her dark, foreign scent, pleasant and strange. I lean in even closer, her black hair tickling my nose, and I inhale. So alluring. Will her rich scent stick to my pillow? Her eyes are closed, dark lashes sticking up like little feelers. Her skin is white in the way we (if there is still a *we* I can claim allegiance to) might find unhealthy but I'm sure she finds healthy and pure. Her lips are stuck together in the corners but parted slightly in the middle, a tiny hole for gentle breathing, vulnerable. She breathes in the air I breathe out. Can she not feel my stares?

My wife's shower faucet squeaks closed. The metal rings slide along the rod. While she pats herself dry (I used to do it for her) I sink my head into the pillow, my nose just barely touching Megumi's tangled hair. I breathe deeply.

The girl bolts upright as though possessed and looks down on me with bulging eyes and her mouth opens but before she makes a sound I put one finger to her lips—so soft—then point to the door, meaning my wife is still here, getting ready for work.

I sit up, and she whispers to me. "What are you doing here?"

I whisper back. "What are *you* doing here?"

She looks into my eyes, dumbfounded. "You were missing," she whispers.

"I'm right here."

Silke's high heels click down the hallway. She knocks on my door. "Thomas, are you awake?"

I find my full voice. "Yes," I say to the door, "I'm awake."

"I'm sorry about last night. I'm not sure what to say, just that I'm sorry. Can you forgive me?"

"Of course," I say, looking at the girl's red mouth, "I forgive you." The girl puts her hand on my leg. A tiny bit of her weight is transferred to me.

"I've been patient, haven't I? I've tried to help you," Silke says. "Have I ever blamed you?"

What have these three years done to her beauty? Her green eyes that used to glow so bright, have they gone dark and sallow? Were she to put her head on my lap, would I find stress wrinkling through her face, would I find gray strands among the gold?

My heart is beginning to swell with uncontrollable, directionless, aimless emotion. I fight it, I squeeze it dry, but it always swells up again, heavy, sodden. I wish the girl weren't here to witness this.

When Silke leaves for work the air clears, the pressure dissipates, but the aftertaste lingers. I make Megumi a cup of microwave coffee, then one for myself. She gulps it down. "I was so worried about you," she says. "Where were you?"

"Pork chops, right? I smelled them when I sneaked in."

"She said you were supposed to come out for dinner."

"It must've been pretty bad last night. She never apologizes."

She searches for clues in my face, something to tell her what is appropriate and what is not. "It's okay," I say, "you can be honest."

She nods her head, her look says it all. I take a sip. My coffee is not as good as Silke's. "I got on a bus," I say. "I rode it back and forth, all night, until I was sure she was asleep."

She pets my beard. "How long has it been since when you shaved?"

"I have no idea. Months and months. A year? Over a year."

Her fingertips worm through my hair and land on my cheeks. She squeezes. "I wonder what you look like under there," she says.

"Don't get your hopes up."

She lets go. "You should let me find out for myself."

In the distance a siren wails. My left arm quivers. I hide it under my back. Ambulances stalk the city, picking up and dropping off. Now another siren joins in, syncopated whoops and chirps, fighting selfish traffic, fighting time.

"Come on," she says, "let's shave it off." She pulls me up by my hands. Our faces are close. Her dark scent. From behind, with her hands on my hips, she steers me to the bathroom.

I stand facing the mirror and she moves left and right in the cramped space, searching for the perfect angle. First, with my orange-handled scissors, she snips away the farthest reaches of my beard. Squiggles float to the floor. "Take off your shirt," she says, but she doesn't wait for me, she pulls it up herself. I reach for the sky.

In the mirror my chest is pale under the bare incandescent light. Not much hair. I used to have more muscle. They have gone a little slack. The contours are subtle now, just enough to remind me what I was. What I could be.

"Have you done this before?" I ask.

"I'll figure it out."

She snips. I suck some squiggles up my nose. It tickles. I sneeze. "Hold still," she says with a smile. "Lean forward," she says, "I'm not that tall." To maintain the position I must brace myself against the sink. "More," she says. The squiggles fall softly, like snow. The scissors open and close with a metallic bite. "You're beginning to take shape," she says. The soft underside of her arm brushes my shoulder, barely a whisper, but my entire body feels it. I get goose bumps. She goes on cutting.

When she is finished trimming she holds a hot, wet towel against my face. Through the towel she massages my cheeks and jaw and forehead. Drops of warm water slide down my chest and disappear into my pants. "Don't you already feel fresher?" she asks.

She pats my cheeks with shaving cream. "It's not foam," I say. "You don't need quite so much."

"It's the good stuff."

"The good stuff? Where do you learn those expressions?"

"I pick them up. I'm always paying some attention." She finishes applying the cream. "Now it's like you have a whole new beard. A snow beard. Maybe this is how you'll look when you're old. Like Santa. Did your father have white hair?"

"My father died before he could go gray."

She tells me I need to hold still. "I don't want to cut your juggler."

"Jugular."

"Just hold still. Did I put on too much cream?"

"Way too much."

"Hold still." She finds the proper angle. She presses the razor to my cheek, up high by the bone. She pulls it down to my jaw. A vertical tract of clear skin surrounded by white. Too much cream. She rinses the blade in the running water. Some of the hairs stick to the porcelain, others plunge down the drain. Blobs of cream stick.

Slowly they erode, lose their grip, and slide down the porcelain into the hole.

Again she sets the razor and pulls. "This is fun," she says. "Are you nervous?"

"Cheeks are the easy part." She sets, she pulls, deliberate and precise. Between my legs it begins to stir. I need a different thought to suppress it. In middle school I'd think about dead cats, piles and piles of dead cats. Worked every time. "Your brother died because he wouldn't accept Japanese blood?"

She rinses the blade and for a few seconds stares into the sink. "No, he died because they forced it into him."

"It was tainted?"

She lines up the next swipe at my face. Her black eyes are complete concentration. I feel as though I am a lump of clay being carved into a sculpture. "Tainted?" she says. "He would've said so. But not like a disease like AIDS. Tainted because it was Japanese. See, my mom isn't Japanese, she's Korean." She flips the razor upside down and starts on my neck. "The thing about Japan is that . . . how do I say it? If an American says he's American, he's talking about the country. About the constitution and the flag and all the amendments. And the founding fathers. But with the Japanese—" She stops to guide the razor up my neck. "If a Japanese says he's Japanese, he's talking more about his blood than the government or the flag. America is values. If you agree to the values and take the tests then you can become American. But in Japan it's not so simple. We have all sorts of labels to describe what kind of Japanese person you are or aren't. Depending on where you were born or who your parents are. Am I explaining this right? Sometimes Americans take it the wrong way. It's all very complicated. I don't even think I could explain it in Japanese."

With a towel she polishes away the mirror's coat of steam. "The other kids, even the parents," she says, "never let us forget we were part Korean. It got pretty bad sometimes."

"What's wrong with Korea?"

"Nothing. But that's not the point."

"So he wanted to be Korean and not Japanese?"

"It's not that, either. He thought of himself as totally Japanese. I do, too. But it was like he wasn't being allowed to be who he felt he was. Not that everyone was mean. Most weren't. But you only pay attention to the mean ones."

"Wasn't it the same for you?"

"He took it harder. We're different. None of that stuff really bothers me. Then again, I wasn't the one who kept getting beaten up because of it. I can't tell you everything that was going on in his head. If I knew maybe I could've done something."

My Adam's apple gives her trouble. She uses short strokes. She tells me to hold my breath. I feel even more like a nascent sculpture, crawling into life from a vacuum. Is this girl my god? Shall I worship her?

She begins on the other cheek. "He didn't want any more Japanese blood," she says, "but they gave it to him anyway. I'm not saying it made sense. I guess it did to him." Tears in her eyes glisten. She wipes them away.

"I'm sorry. You don't have to tell me if you don't want."

Again she rubs away the steam. She pulls the razor across my cheek and even with all that cream it sounds like sandpaper. "He had been back from the hospital for three days. By the time I got home from school that afternoon the men in yellow jumpsuits were cleaning it up. His body was gone. Mom was crying. Dad was staring out the window at a pine tree." She holds my chin in her fingertips and turns my face left, then right, then left, then right. "When was the last time someone kissed your smooth cheek?"

She slices away the last of my beard. "When they finally let me in his room, it was so strange. It was perfectly clean, like nothing happened. The yellow jumpsuits erased what he did. They erased my brother. Mom told me how she found him. He was naked in the middle of the floor. The whole floor was a pool of dark red. He finally drained out all that Japanese blood."

She massages my face again with a steaming towel. I close my eyes and plunge into the moment. Let it never end.

"Thomas, you're beautiful." I roll my eyes in an exaggerated way: I can't afford to let her know that I believe she means it. "Is it weird to say? I just mean that it's a transformative."

"Transformation. And it's not. It's just a shave."

"But you're a whole new person. I did good, didn't I? Not even a scratch."

We lie next to each other on the bed. My shirt is back on. My face feels fresh. She might be right about me being a new person. "Do you talk to my wife?"

"No, not really. Sometimes."

"She used to bring men to the apartment," I say. The girl takes my hand. I can feel her pulse. If we held each other tight enough, would our beating hearts synchronize?

"You heard them?"

"She'd leave the door open."

"Did you ever go out there?"

"And do what?"

"She wants attention."

My wife must have expected that in my room Megumi's and my feelings would tangle. Did she decide it was worth the risk? Is she confident that, whatever happens, she will win out in the end, or does she not care about any of that and just wants me to be out in the world again, even if it's not with her?

"Anything you want," Megumi is saying. "I'll go get it." I harbor no specific cravings, or more precisely, I deny myself cravings that can only go unfulfilled.

"Roast beef and Swiss," I finally say, "Lettuce, tomato, onion, mayo. Lots of mayo. Salt and pepper. On a hero."

It's ridiculous that while she is out getting lunch I am lonely, yet here I am at the window, shade pulled back, peeking down at the empty street, waiting, wasting no opportunity to catch a glimpse. I try the bed, but her absence, her lingering wake, consumes me. My gaze ricochets off the walls. Back at the window I stare into the distance. How far away is the sky?

It's even more ridiculous that a roast beef sandwich could reduce me to tears, yet here I am. Just my right eye, not my left. I can barely swallow.

"What's wrong?" she says when she gets back.

I shake my head. We eat on the floor, our heros unwrapped, the white paper forming our placemats. We dump our chips into a pile. I drink a can of Coke. She drinks ginger ale. Between us are pickles. I imagine that we are sitting in the grass, on the bank of a slow river.

"I know what you're doing," I say. "Do you really think a sandwich will make me long for the world?"

"I just thought you might want some lunch." She tries a bite of my roast beef. I try a bite of her ham and egg and tomato. "It's really warm out today," she says. "Like spring. I wish you could've come with me. It'd be fun to walk together."

The afternoon unwinds. The window burns golden. She runs her fingers across my new face and says my skin is smooth. Her fingers are just as smooth. Smoother.

"I told you about my brother. Tell me about your son."

"I killed him." Looking into the mirror after she shaved me was like rummaging through the dark corner of a forgotten drawer and discovering an old photograph.

"You didn't. If you killed him, you'd be in jail."

"What do you think this is?"

She sits on the bed. I lie with my head on her lap. With her fingertips she inspects my hair and ear and neck. I don't mind. The late afternoon sun has sunk and shines directly through the window, casting a wide beam of light across the wood floor, a beam of brilliance that suddenly appears and disappears with the stray passing of clouds.

I am falling, no doubt, the ground beneath me has crumbled away and I am swallowed into the blackness, and nothing's left for me but to fall, to feel the wind in my face, to resign myself to the depths, and I wonder if there ever really was any solid ground beneath my feet, or if I was perched on the tiny tip of a thousand-foot needle, balancing way up high, appearing still and solid and steady, but constantly contracting my muscles in perfect orchestration to keep my balance, lest the slightest breeze knock me over. The girl sent me falling. I reach out, but my arms are mercilessly short and there is nothing to grab to break my plunge, only the air itself, slipping through my fingers as I squeeze. But at this moment, I have nothing to fear. At this exact moment I am not so much falling as floating—so long is the shaft through which I descend—the wind through my hair, my stomach queasy, bobbing in a void. How long since I last felt so free? My muscles need not contract endlessly now, I can finally relax. I hope I land in some soft place, or even better that I never land, that this falling becomes my new state of being.

"My neighbor Morris's son was teaching my son how to draw pictures on the sidewalk with colored chalk. Houses and trees and the sun and dinosaurs. I sipped Silke's coffee out of a mug we bought in Paris. She was supposed to come down when she was off the phone. It's funny the things you remember. I had one shoelace untied. I was wearing these old ratty sneakers—cross-country racers, actually—leftovers from college. They fit like slippers. I know for sure one was untied but I can't remember which one, and when I imagine it in my mind and look down at my shoes, sometimes I see the left one untied, and sometimes the right one. Anyway, then we heard a cardinal up in the maple tree. I heard a cardinal but Morris heard only a bird. *What's that,* he said. *A bird,* I said. *No shit,* he said, *what kind of bird? Don't swear in front of my kid,* I said, *and it's a cardinal.* We peered into the leaves, trying to find the bird, and finally there she was, a gray female cardinal, singing away on a Saturday morning. Then, such a sickening noise, the screech of rubber against pavement. So loud, so close. A woman screamed. And just like that it was over, no sounds of any kind, no song, no screech, no scream. A frozen moment."

I couldn't believe what I was seeing then. It could not be real. Not a denial of what I know to be the truth, not that kind of disbelief, but something much deeper: the complete inability to comprehend that such a sight was even possible, within the laws of physics or any other law by which real things happen.

"That stupid cardinal. We took our eyes off our kids for what, thirty seconds? Thirty seconds of looking at a cardinal. Now, of course, after replaying it over and over in my mind I see that the cardinal was giving me a warning. From high on her perch she saw my son run into the road and she saw the speeding car close the gap. She was telling me to look out, to protect my child. She was a siren, and I just stared at her, listening to her song, not doing a goddamned thing, like I was staring up in amazement at a screaming smoke detector in the middle of the room, surrounded by flames, oblivious.

"Silke screamed from upstairs in the window, and the frozen moment was over. The white mug from Paris crashed to the cement. I leapt down the steps and into the street. My son lay on the road, bloody, barely conscious."

I kneeled over him and held his hand and touched his face. That's the right thing to do, isn't it? We're told not to move the victim, it's better to wait for the professionals. My son wasn't crying, just groaning, and barely. From the looks of him, an impartial observer might have said it was already too late. What could the professionals do? Send the professionals back, no need for them here. Send them somewhere they might do some good. Not here. Too late.

"But I was not an impartial observer. I debated: maybe if I picked him up so carefully and took him into my arms and hugged him hard enough I could squeeze out all the hurt. I heard a siren off in the distance.

"Silke rushed down and we became mirror images of each other. I was on my knees and held his right hand and gently stroked his forehead full of cuts. She knelt on the other side, holding his left hand and stroking his forehead. The siren grew louder but never seemed to come. I held his hand as he lay dying. The driver of the car stood behind Silke, bawling, hysterical, horrified at what she had done, and I remember thinking she had chosen the perfect spot to stand: not too far away, as though she weren't responsible, as though she were trying to escape the scene, and not too close that she was intruding on us, who wanted nothing to do with her. There was only one spot that fulfilled those requirements and she was standing on it. Some human instinct drove her there. She was the only one crying. I wasn't crying. Silke wasn't crying. I had to lean in close to hear his fading gurgles. We were so focused on comforting him we didn't think to cry. Soothing words, soothing touches, that's all we could offer."

"It's okay it's okay it's okay, I said, stroking his forehead even as he spit up blood, running out the corner of his mouth and down his chin and cheek, and I had an instinct—my left arm actually twitched—to pick up his bib and wipe off the blood as though it were pureed peas. But he wasn't wearing his bib, and it wasn't pureed peas.

"The paramedics said, 'Stand back, please.' And just like that our jobs as parents were over."

Stand back, please. You're no longer needed.

Fifteen

SHE ORDERS THAI FOR dinner. I give her cash and she goes to the front door. When I suggested Japanese food she puckered her face and said the Japanese food here is no good.

We share everything. Tom yum soup. Pad thai. Sour sausage with raw onions and raw ginger and peanuts. Panang curry. We go back and forth between the dishes. "How come Americans don't like to share their food?" she says. "In my country we are always sharing. Korea, too. One big pot in the middle. But Americans need their own plates of food. Even if two people order the same thing, they each need their own private plate. Why is that?"

"I've never thought about it. Is that true?"

"Except for pizza. Pizza is the only thing I've seen Americans eat like Asians. A big pizza in the middle and everyone takes a slice when they need it. And pizza is America's favorite food, but why don't they like to share anything else?"

"Americans like their own."

Megumi is still in my room when my wife returns. "What's that smell?" she says from the hallway. "Did you get food delivered?"

"Thai food," I say.

"And you came out to get it?"

"I went down to the front door."

A stiff silence. I wait. Disbelievers don't always reveal their suspicion. Layers of lies, back and forth.

"Sweetie," she says, "I'm proud of you. It's Megumi, right? She's helping you emerge. Any leftovers for me?"

"I was so hungry. Sorry."

"I'm sure you were."

Hours pass. My wife shuts off the television and goes to bed. She cries. Her door is open. We lie together on the bed and listen to her sobs. It's like the nights after his death, when Silke and I lay in bed next to each other, wide awake in the dark, listening for the other to fall asleep but saying not a word.

I wake up in the middle of the night. Megumi's hand is on me. I keep my eyes closed. She explores. Perhaps she, too, is only half awake. The blanket shifts.

It starts as a single spot of warmth. Her tongue and hands work in concert, improvising. I keep my eyes pinched shut. The warmth spreads, slowly.

She pulls my hand to her breast. Her nipple is thick. I pinch. She makes a sound. There is no me anymore, no skin, no bones, no guts. There is only warmth.

I peek. The whites of her eyes flash up at me. Pure white surrounding circles of pure black, a void. It is enough for me to finish. She waits until she has it all, then she waits longer, until her warm mouth puts me asleep, until I fade away.

In the morning, Silke's knocking wakes me. She calls out my name. "Maybe tonight when I get back from work you can come out and we can sit on the sofa and watch a movie. Wouldn't that be nice?"

My voice refuses me.

"Think about it, okay?"

Megumi showers. She comes out of the bathroom already dressed, offering me no naked glimpse. "How about some coffee?" she says. I head toward the microwave. "No," she says, "I mean real coffee. I'll go out and get it." She puts on her coat and a pair of blue mittens. But at the door she stops. "Come with me."

"I'm not dressed."

"It's okay, I'll wait."

In return for the warmth she gave me last night, I owe it to her to go get coffee, that is the deal, that is the give and take between people, the beginning of the tangled knots. "I can't," I say.

"Please? It's just around the corner. I really want you to come with me."

"You're so demanding," I say in what I hope comes off as a playful voice. It's been a while since I've made these kinds of inflections. I'm sure it sounds a little off, but I keep trying. "You know what I used to call you before I even met you, when you first came to my door?"

"You didn't call me anything. You just stayed so quiet."

"No, I mean what I called you to myself. In my head. I called you my pest. Actually I didn't call you *my* pest. I just called you a pest. Because you were one."

She comes over and straddles me, then makes her arms into a life preserver and drops them onto my shoulders. She looks me right in the eye. "But now I'm *your* pest?"

"Maybe."

"That's all you called me, your pest?"

"Lately I've been saying pretty little pest."

"But am I *your* pretty little pest?" She tightens her hold, pulling me closer. She kisses my neck and jumps off my lap. "No answer? Well think about it while I get the coffee. I'll be right back. Don't go anywhere. I'll expect an answer," she says, smiling.

Time is seeping in, pushing into my room, collecting on the walls like condensation, the drops touching and growing larger, out of control. My life is no longer a hovering point. When she is gone, I am anxious for her return.

What I did to my son is unforgivable. The car came speeding around the corner. It was the one moment, above all others, that I should have been a father. But I did not leap into action, into the road; I did not scoop him into my arms and hold him tight and scold him by saying, "What did I tell you about running into the street?" He didn't live long enough for me to scold him.

Instead I waited for my instincts to kick in and catapult me into automatic, thoughtless, selfless action. I sat on the top step as the scene unfolded, waiting for the instinct, the instinct that makes us human, the instinct that says we must protect the ones we love, the ones for whom we are responsible. But that instinct never came.

The implications are too horrifying to face.

She returns to my room, but she has no coffee. Tears and blood run down her cheek. One eye is swollen.

She sits on my bed, hiding in her hands. "What happened to you?" She turns away. "Let me see."

She tells me she's sorry. "I should get going," she says.

"No. Stay. What happened? Did someone do this to you?" I go to the window. The street is empty.

She takes another shower. The wait is unbearable. My insides churn and wrench. True feelings emerge when you see someone suffer. There is no denying them. The sight of her pain sickens me. And once again I am too late to help, to prevent, to protect. I did nothing. I wasn't where I was supposed to be. I should've gone with her.

I pace the room. Out the window, the street is lifeless. Nothing moves. Both hands burrow through my hair and squeeze my head to contain the pressure. The water drops explode against the porcelain. But propriety says I must stay out here and wait. She needs time to be alone.

The water stops. "Are you okay?"

"Do you have any bandages?"

"Can I come in?"

She opens the door. She has a towel wrapped over her chest. My towel. I rummage through the drawer. "Sit on the toilet," I say. A single gash cuts across her cheek, washed clean but still seeping blood, split wider from the pressure. I select the appropriate size and carefully cover the wound. A purple bruise bulges from under the bandage. She looks up at me with a heartbreaking expression. "I guess I really am a pest," she says.

I kiss her bruised cheek. A dome of angry blood.

"Do you have a sweatshirt or something?" she says. I find one and turn away as she changes. The towel drops to the floor. "I'm so stupid," she says.

My sweatshirt is too big for her. It looks like a thick hooded dress.

She lies down on my bed and burrows under the covers. "Megumi, what happened?" I repeat. I am suddenly jealous of people who can pronounce her name perfectly.

"I've been through worse than this. I'll be okay," she says.

"Let me help you."

"You have. You are. I'm supposed to be the one helping you. I'm so embarrassed. Don't worry. Okay?"

"Tell me what happened."

"Your neighbor."

"Morris?"

She nods. "I just want to sleep for a time."

She is curled into a ball beneath my sheets. I sit at the window. Fresh air swirls in. The maple tree trembles. The bandage bisects her cheek. The bruise will take time to fade completely into her pristine face. Without waking, she pulls the hood over her head. The scar might never go away.

Again I caused pain. I sent her to her fate. I refused to move. Are my feelings so important that I must allow them to cause pain?

Fifteen minutes should be okay. It's the least I could do. I quietly put on my jacket and shoes. I leave a note, just in case. *I'll be right back.*

Outside, I look into Morris's windows. Nothing. A mother and her child walk toward me. They pass without looking at me. I press Morris's bell. He does not answer. The knob does not budge. There

will be another time. I am a patient man. As I walk down the block
I hope he is spying on me from the window, that he knows it was me
at his door, that he knows I know what he did.

The cashier greets me with a smile, as though I am normal.
The air is stained with coffee. I find my voice and place my order.
I breathe in the coffee air and hold it. My cheeks tingle. My second time outside this week, both times in daylight. I feel like a sail
unfurling.

As I climb my front steps, I again look into Morris's windows.
The blinds are closed now. I hold my stare and hope he is watching
me through one of the gaps.

Megumi is uncurled, awake, still wearing only my sweatshirt.
"Coffee delivery," I say. She lowers the hood and fixes her hair. She
smiles. We drink the coffee on the bed. "I got doughnuts, too. Do
you like doughnuts?"

"Yum, who doesn't like doughnuts?" She tests the temperature
with her lips. She drinks. We pass a doughnut back and forth. "Japanese even share doughnuts?" I say.

"It's my fault," she says. "I shouldn't have gone over there. I
should've known better. But I thought I could handle it." She tells
me how Morris asked her to come inside, that he was concerned
about me and that he offered to help. Showed her pictures of his wife
and son. "He said your sons were close."

"They played together sometimes, that's all."

"He said you were best friends."

"We were neighbors."

"He told me he knew why I was coming to see you. I told him he had the wrong idea. I tried to leave but he grabbed me."

She says Morris had her arm. She pulled and pulled but didn't scream. She tried making her way toward the door, but he kept pulling her arm. He told her that they had plenty of time before his wife came home, and that if she does that psycho Thomas, why won't she do him?

"His wife?" I say. "She's dead. Cancer."

"He told me she was at work. He held on and I pulled, and then suddenly he let go and I fell and my face hit the table. I came straight here."

"And that's everything that happened?"

She nods. "But if Morris was your friend at all, if he knows you're up here, then why didn't he try to help you? And you must've had other friends, too."

"At first, maybe. But grief and guilt as deep as mine, people see it and run the other way. I think they were somehow relieved I wouldn't come out—saved them from having to avoid me. Like how nobody gets too close to a vagrant. It's just an instinct people have, I guess, to stay away from grief and guilt."

She pulls me on top of her. What's left of my coffee spills and soaks through the sheets. Her lips taste like coffee and sugar.

I wonder if this is my wife's intent, if she told the girl to do whatever it takes to get me out, or if maybe these kisses are real. They feel real.

She takes off the sweatshirt. She squeezes her breast and pulls my mouth to it.

I take off my clothes. She no longer needs to pull me. My naked body remembers now what to do. She is so young, her appetite immense. She devours me. Her eagerness awakens me. The dark foreign scent that stuck to my pillow, it covers her entire body, every curve and surface. It is not just a scent. It is a flavor.

I am embarrassed. I have no stamina. She's too much. Every time I push the impulse down it surges up stronger. I hold perfectly still. "Don't stop," she says. She wraps her arms around me. Not a single space exists between us.

I am careful not to rupture her bruised cheek. A small red splotch of blood seeps through the bandage. My failure.

There's no stopping it this time. At a certain point the force continues forward regardless of my wishes. The most determined will is powerless against it. It's a force of nature in the most violent, beautiful, uncontrollable sense. It puts us in our place. I start to pull out, but she clamps her thighs around me like a vice. Her legs are steel. "Don't go," she says. Our convulsions flow through each other in waves. She says something in Japanese and hugs me tighter. Even when I finish she doesn't let go. Our breathing synchronizes, slower and slower, like dying music.

My nose grazes her neck. Her neck is wet. I kiss it. She puts her hand on my head. I kiss it again. "I ruined your bed with the coffee," she says.

I sleep deeply, too deep for dreams. When I wake, my head is still on her shoulder. She is staring up at the ceiling. "What's it like when you have sex with me?" she says. Her hair tickles my face.

I may have just created a life, something I vowed never again to do. They are swimming inside her now, beyond my reach. They are on their own now. I can only wait. Three years of resolve, shattered. What use is resolve?

She kisses my chest. The tip of her tongue licks my skin. "You're salty," she says. "Have you ever slept with a Japanese girl?"

"No."

"Is it different?"

Her breathing grows louder. She is sleeping. A string of drool spills out the corner of her mouth and lands on my chest. The red splotch on her bandage has turned brown. Once, twice, her foot jerks. Then her shoulders. I try to imagine her dream.

My mind races. My thinking is clear but aimless. Thoughts pour in and out before I can catch them. I used to fantasize that I was a caterpillar and this room my chrysalis. I'd fantasize about my metamorphosis, about the day I'd emerge. Then I realized that this room is not a chrysalis, that it is isolation, banishment. But now a naked girl is sleeping on my chest, so I can hardly be called an isolate. So, if not a chrysalis and if not banishment, then what is my room?

"You blame yourself, don't you?" she says, upon awakening.

"I shouldn't have sent you out there alone. I should have gone with you." I try to land my gaze on her eyes, but the angle isn't right. I can only see the top of her head and her bare shoulder.

"You're very kind. But I meant your son. You blame yourself."

The room grows darker. The sun is setting. It's sad how in winter the sun's arc is so low in the sky, no energy to go higher. A gentle lob. "Of course I blame myself. But it's worse than that. When the car sped down the street, I discovered I'm a monster."

She tells me I'm not a monster. Says that the way I bandaged her cheek was gentle. My neighbor, she says, is a monster.

"There are different kinds of monsters," I say.

I was tested. Until that Saturday morning, I had rolled through life, and my good persona was the aggregate of millions of inconsequential decisions. But my true character lurked, it hid behind the good grades and Valentine's Day dinners and professional success, and later it lurked behind the words I heard all the time: *You're a good father.*

We'd been over it before, dozens of times—no running into the road. He repeated it back to me. He even pulled on my hand when he saw some other kids running into the street and said to me, "Why don't their dads tell them it's dangerous?" I thought he understood. I thought I had been a good teacher. My job was to make sure he survived his mistakes, so that he could learn and grow. But I fell short. My son didn't survive my failure.

Everyone told me it wasn't my fault, that there was nothing I could've done. It happened too fast, they said. Even Morris said that it all happened in an instant. But they don't know that their instant was my eternity. Time stopped. The car, the singing cardinal, my son, everything froze but me. I was free to move about that frozen world at my own pace. I could've taken a sip of coffee, stood up, stretched, then strolled into the road, picked him up and scolded him for running into the street, for breaking the rules. I could've set him back on the sidewalk and sat down for more coffee. Plenty of time.

I looked at the speeds and trajectories; I did the geometry, the physics, and it all added up: the car would hit my son. I could've acted quickly and decisively. There was time. I would like to excuse myself by saying my muscles refused me. But my muscles stood ready. My mind refused me. And what about my heart? I did not push him out of the way; I did not trade my life for his. I didn't even scream. Instinct never found me.

Everyone felt so sorry for us, for me. They came to us; they helped. They said they'd give us whatever we needed. In their eyes we were just as much victims as he was. He had lost, but we had suffered his loss. Their sympathy was overwhelming and touching. Humiliating. I was drowning in a deep sea of sympathy, choking on the salt.

What kind of father lacks this prime instinct? What kind of husband?

The girl strokes my arm. "I can't let it happen again," I say. "I'm a bad person."

"You're a good person. Bad people never think they're bad."

We are still in bed when my wife returns home. It's nearly midnight. Megumi suddenly sits up and points to her bare feet. Her face is urgent. I crawl down and plant a kiss on her big toe. Even her toes are soft and fresh. She shakes her head. She stabs again at her feet and whispers into my ear, "My shoes are out there."

We whisper behind my closed bathroom door. "I can't believe it," she says. "I'm normally so careful."

"It's Morris. You were upset. You forgot. It's not your fault."

"My whole life I've come home and kicked off my shoes."

"It's okay."

"She saw them. She knows I'm here."

We put on our clothes. "Maybe you could go out now," I say. "You could tell her it's just a normal visit. Give her a progress report."

"I can't face her."

"Maybe she didn't see them. And even if she did, you're not doing anything wrong. Maybe she's just giving us space, letting you do your work."

"Then shouldn't we be talking, making some noise? The quiet is suspicious."

We spend the night in harsh silence. The silence is a solid mass, suffocating every space, no room to breathe.

She falls asleep with her head on my shoulder. When I am sure Silke has also fallen asleep, I sneak out and retrieve Megumi's shoes. They are small.

In the morning the sun is shining. I make two cups of microwave coffee. Megumi wears one of my black T-shirts. She asks me to crack open the window.

"I thought you said you left your shoes by the front door. But you meant my bedroom door."

"No, the front door. What are you talking about?"

"They weren't at the front door. They were sitting right outside my door."

"I didn't put them there."

Sixteen

"WHAT HAPPENED TO YOU?" Hamamoto says with the innocent worry of a friend, but Megumi knows that suspicion fuels her concern.

"I fell and hit a coffee table."

"Let me take a look." Hamamoto inspects her cheek, looking for signs of a lie. Later in the day she asks about Thomas. Megumi gives all the right answers.

"Can you get him out?"

"Yes. It will take some more time, but I can do it."

"His wife called me. She's not in a good state. I'm afraid that she . . . Megumi, you need to hurry. Do whatever you can to get him out. I wish we could force him, that's how bad I think it is with Silke. He needs to come out."

When the shop closes, she goes home. Her apartment has never felt so lonely. It is a waste that she and Thomas should both be alone. The worst kind of loneliness is when you're unable to be where you want to be, where you wouldn't have to be alone.

She opens a Kirino novel but can't read more than a few paragraphs before drifting to his dark, round eyes, an image that is no mere memory, something apart from herself, capable of being remembered or forgotten, kept or discarded; rather, his eyes looking down at her have woven their way into her internal fabric, inseparable from the rest. And last night, in the silence of his room, the distance between them shrank down to nothing. He took care of her the way she once took care of her brother.

The clock on the wall ticks steadily. She watches the long hand sweep around the dial, not smoothly, but in rests and leaps. Maybe during one of the rests between the leaps Thomas sat paralyzed as the car hit his son. And maybe during one of the rests her brother sliced himself. Do everybody's rests and leaps align, or are we missing each other?

Her father calls. "I have the most wonderful news," he says, and his voice is filled with life. Gone is the begging, the bitterness. Swept away, replaced with light. "It's about your mother," he says, and the word stings her throat, a hive of bees, the mother she hasn't heard from in over three years, who fled Japan in despair. "Here," he says, "I'll let her tell you for herself."

Tell you for herself? The words don't even register before her mother greets her in Korean-tinged Japanese, a casual *Moshi moshi* as though they saw each other just yesterday. "Moshi moshi," her mother repeats into the silence. "Megumi, are you there?" But her mouth is dry as dust. "Megumi?" Her cheeks grow hot, then numb.

"Yes, Mother, I'm here." She says it quietly, respectfully, to this ghost of a mother. Ashen tongue, she nearly chokes.

"You're there, but I'm here, so why are you there instead of here?" her mother says with a girl's giddy brightness.

"Mother?" She tells her mother that she doesn't understand. She asks what she's doing in Japan, why she's not still in Korea.

"Your father wanted me to keep it a secret until we were two hundred percent sure. I've been here a few weeks."

She puts her fingers to her cheeks—still numb and hot. "Until you're sure of what?"

"Of each other and you and everything. Megumi, it's time to come home."

"You're back together?"

"And we want you to come back." She always thought her mother's Japanese was special, her odd grammar mixed with Korean sounds and inflections but at times perfectly correct and natural, a breed of Japanese that only she will ever speak, and now Megumi's hearing it again when she least expected, when she thought she never again would. She suddenly wonders what Thomas thinks about her own unique English. Is the sound of her English music to his ears? ". . . and we've moved into a different home. A fresh start."

"Mom, I don't know, I . . . don't you still—"

"You're my daughter. That will never change."

"And I'm supposed to come back home, just like that?" Three years of loneliness, no family, of hovering between the past and the future, unsure where to land.

"And there's one more thing," her mother says. "You have a new baby brother."

Seventeen

HER INTENTION WAS TO sneak past sleeping Silke. Now she's not so sure. She sits on the stoop across from his building. His light is on. A cat crosses the road. It makes no sound, paws barely touching the ground, gliding, disappearing into a thin black space between two buildings. She watches, wondering if another might follow. Nothing. She is alone. She fills her lungs with air, holds it for a moment, then lets out a deep, humid breath. She puts her hands together and slips them between her knees. Morris's windows are dark.

She didn't know what else to do, where else to go, she couldn't keep pacing her apartment, ticking clock, she needed to get out. She ran to the M20 uptown bus. To her right, Central Park was a long stone wall and a black snarl of trees.

"For so long I've been dying to tell you," her mother said. When she left Japan she didn't know she was pregnant. She had thought she'd never be able to have another child.

"And you've been raising him by yourself in Korea this whole time?"

"I'm not going to explain everything now," she said. "We can talk about it when you come back. We're a family again. I've told your brother all about his beautiful sister. He can't wait to meet you."

Then her father took the phone. "Isn't it wonderful? Here— someone wants to say 'Hi.' He's been practicing."

She almost hung up. Quick, before it's real, hang up! she told herself. Quick! Now!

But she waited. She heard her mother's gentle prompting in the background.

"Noona?" he said in Korean, and then in Japanese, *"Oneesan?" Big sister?* An hour later her tears had still not stopped.

As she sits on a stoop across the street from Thomas's room, her brother's tiny voice echoes in her mind. Will he grow up smart? Strong?

The people in her life, every one of them, have been living these three years separately, apart, alone. Silke, Thomas, her father, her mother and brother, herself. How will the dots reconnect, and in what direction, old or new? She has no true need to return to Japan. Her mother and father are perfectly capable of tending to her brother, of giving him food and clothes and shelter. But—half Korean, half Japanese—who will help him grow up proud?

The clock ticks in her head. Louder. Louder. Rests and leaps. It's afternoon in Tokyo. What is her brother, her new brother, doing? Playing? Eating a treat?

She shivers. Not from the biting air, but from the sudden memory of her older brother on the first day of his first year of high school, when he came home with cuts all over his face and bruises all over his arms and back and chest. A patch of hair was torn out and his head was bleeding. They wanted to send him a message: He's impure. He's less. Anyone whose father turned his back on his people deserved to be beaten.

They were starting dinner and he walked into the kitchen and just stood there. On display. The blood on his face was dried, but on top of the dried blood new shiny blood was oozing out. Nobody at the table moved. Her mom began to push back her chair, but her brother shook his head and motioned for everyone to stay where they were. Megumi was afraid to swallow her mouthful of rice. It might make too much noise. His shirt was torn and stained with dirt and blood and slowly he unbuttoned it. It fell to the floor. Then he turned around slowly and stuck out his arms. His back and chest and arms were swollen and purple. He was lean and muscular but not very big, and she wondered how many people it had taken to do this to him. If he fought back. Or if he just sat there and took the beating. He didn't say a word.

Her mother couldn't look at him anymore. She just stared into her miso soup, at the floating seaweed. Her dad got up but her brother pushed him away and went into the bathroom. She swallowed her rice, followed him into the bathroom, and closed the door. He stood there for a while, looking at himself in the mirror. His eyes didn't appear to be in focus, and the left one was swollen almost shut. He kept staring into the mirror. He didn't seem to be in pain. He seemed numb, empty, as though the punches hadn't hurt him but instead had sucked the life out of him.

She took some fresh towels from the cupboard and put some warm water in the sink. She sat him down on the floor stool and cleaned up his face and his head, where the hair was torn out. His skin smelled of sweat and blood. Dirt and oil. She looked up to him, but at that moment he was like a baby, helpless. She filled the tub with hot water and took off his pants and socks and pulled off his underwear. Then she took off all her clothes. She gave him a good shower. She scrubbed off all the dirt and blood and oil. It looked like he had been rolling on the ground, like everyone had taken turns kicking him. He stood there while she washed his hair and cleansed his body. She scrubbed everywhere. She was gentle. But she couldn't scrub off the purple and yellow and red bruises. She heard their parents arguing out in the kitchen, trying to whisper.

Each member of the family was so different from the others. Mom and Dad on one side, she and her brother on the other. But even Mom and Dad were different from each other. A family of one Japanese, one Korean, and two mutts. It's strange to be different from your parents, who are different from each other.

After she cleaned and rinsed him, she led him into the bath. While he soaked, she showered. Sometimes she took the bowl and poured hot water through his hair. He reached his hand out of the water, and she held it. He never said a word. Just before the water turned cool, she guided him out of the tub and dried him with a towel. She brushed his teeth. He did the rinsing and spitting; she did the brushing. He was waking up a bit. He watched her as she bandaged his cuts. She dressed him in his *yukata*. She put hers on, too.

She took him to his room and put him into bed. She asked him if he wanted her to stay with him. He took her face in his hands and smiled and shook his head.

That's how it started. The next morning he said through the door he was in too much pain and couldn't go to school. He said he wasn't going back until he was all healed.

She didn't think anything was wrong at first. But then one day when she went to rebandage his wounds he wouldn't let her in.

She left the fresh bandages and medicines on the floor outside his door.

For a couple of weeks he'd come out only for dinner, but he'd just play with his food, eat a few bites and go back to his room. He wouldn't say anything and he wouldn't look at them. The silences were heavy and tense. After a while, maybe a month, they started talking at dinner as though it was just the three of them, as if it was a family of three, plus a pet who ate at the table. Eventually he stopped even coming out. Her mother put a tray at the door for him, like a dog.

Megumi sometimes went to his door, but all he'd say was, "I'm not healed yet. I'll come out when I'm healed." Months and months of the same. Then her mother stopped putting food at the door. He was on his own.

Thomas's light is still on. There is no silhouette, just the steady glow. Silke's window is dark.

She can't be alone; she needs more than memories. Alone is harsh. Alone is loud. Thomas is warm and still.

The stairway up to his fifth-floor apartment has the slightly burnt smell of lingering cooking. She puts her ear to the door. She turns the key. She turns the knob.

The living room is dark. She suddenly can't remember the place-ment of the furniture. She holds still. Her eyes adjust. Shadows be-gin to form, outlines, delineating objects from empty space. From her purse she takes a scrap of paper and writes a quick note, as best she can in the dark, by feel. She takes off her shoes and holds them. Her bare feet stick to the wood floor. The piano sits silent.

Silke's door is open. The hallway seems endless. She does not peek inside as she passes. She slides the note under his door and knocks, barely.

The strip of light beneath his door vanishes. He opens the door. He pulls her in by the hand. The locks snap tight. He keeps her hand. He kisses her. His lips are warm. She is floating. The whole world is black.

"Are you okay?" he says into her ear. His voice tickles.

"I just wanted to see you," she says.

The light comes on. The world reappears, solid. Stacks of boxes. Bed, desk, dresser, microwave, refrigerator. Magazines. Two lamps. Television.

He kisses the tiny button of a bruise. "Can we get out of here?" she says. The room is too small. "Just for an hour. Will you come walk with me?"

"She's a light sleeper."

"We can make it."

He goes to the window and pulls back the shade. Looks the street up and down. "I could use some groceries," he says.

The ritual begins. The door open just a crack. The listening, the crouching. He leads her by the hand past his wife's room.

Outside, there is no breeze. They walk in silence. He's not used to walking with another person and sometimes he bumps into her. They walk according to separate rhythms.

A car speeds toward them, its engine sound increasing in pitch as it closes the gap. As it passes it looks completely mechanical, an autonomous robot creature rolling down the road. The pitch of the engine grows lower as it leaves them behind. "Do you hear that?" she says. "It's called the Doppler effect. My brother taught me about it. He said that to determine if two bodies are moving farther apart or closer together, all you have to do is listen."

This is the deepest part of night, when the day has finally wound completely down, when everything is for a few moments perfectly still before winding back up again. For these few moments the world seems in perfect balance. A lonely sparrow chirps, awake too early.

"In America they say that birds sing," she says. "But in Korea they say that birds cry. Do you know why? It's because of the Japanese ... how can I say it? Because of all the Japanese soldiers in Korea during the world war."

"Occupation."

"The story is that Korean birds used to sing, but when the Japanese soldiers came they started to cry. Even now when Koreans hear birds they say *'Saega ooleo.' The birds are crying.*"

"Why did you leave Japan? What happened?"

They pass closed shops and dark windows. The sky shows no sign of turning brighter. But she knows the sun will eventually rise and she will have to leave Thomas and go back to work selling wagashi. She wishes the sun would stay sunken.

"I had this idea that . . . that if I could make enough money, I could take my brother out of his room and move away to America or Australia. Some place where being half Korean didn't matter. I thought I could save him. I thought we could start fresh. It was my last year of high school and my parents wanted me to go to college, but how could I go when I knew my brother was in his room like that? So I started meeting clients. Men."

The money she earned from selling her panties wasn't enough to take her brother away from Japan. So she bought some plain white silky fabric, cut out little rectangles, folded the rectangles in half, and sewed them into her panties. Labels. On the back of the labels she wrote her cell phone number discreetly. The Agency would never know.

Most guys never called. She'd write her phone number, drop her panties into the pretty box at the Agency, take her envelope with the ¥10,000 and never hear from the pervert who purchased them. She had expected every guy to see her number and call right away. If they wanted her panties, they must—once given the option—also want her, right? She was diving into the thick sludge of men's perversions, and she was getting stuck.

Then one day during biology class her cell phone vibrated inside her backpack. After class she pulled it out and found someone had texted I HAVE YOUR PANTIES.

She texted back: WANNA MEET? The reply was immediate.

She texted him to go to a certain Shibuya love hotel, on the hill, at exactly four o'clock (couldn't stay out too late on a school night, had to be home for dinner), no earlier, no later. She added that the cost was ¥60,000, an inconceivable amount of money, a ridiculous amount of money, an amount she never thought she'd get away with.

At 3:50 p.m., from across the street and around a corner, she staked out the love hotel. Nobody went in or out until exactly four o'clock, when a man walked in, nervously glancing over his shoulder to see if he had been spotted. It was a self-service hotel, so she figured five minutes would be all it would take for him to get settled in a room.

From across the street he hadn't looked like a pervert. He looked like any other guy: tired, slouched, slightly sad. He wore a dark suit and tie, he didn't look crazy, and he wasn't as old as she had expected. Old, but not that old. Just a random guy she might one day find herself waiting behind in line at a store. Or at the table next to hers in a restaurant. Or the father of one of her friends from school.

After five minutes, she texted him: WHICH ROOM? She went inside and knocked on the door to room 15, and the man who had purchased her panties let her in.

It surprised her so few men contacted her through her labels. She had figured she'd have to sleep with hundreds of men, each once. Instead, few men called but those who did wanted to see her regularly, so over the next year and a half, while her brother was living in his room, she had a constant stable of clients. One or two would fade away just as one or two new ones contacted her. It worked out.

The money piled up. Payment for services rendered.

The sex was mostly boring, but there's nothing wrong with being bored, and sometimes the sex was good—men and their fantasies— once in a while even great, and some men seemed to save their best sex for her, as though they had something to prove. What that something to prove might be she had no idea, but she was certain these men didn't fuck their wives the way they fucked her.

Mostly though, the biggest obstacle to overcome was the sadness. All those men carried with them profound sadness, often buried deep deep deep, but visible to her. After sex, spent and looking up at the ceiling, the men let down their guard and the sadness came oozing out. This, the hardest part: to ignore the sadness, to not reach out, to not become involved, to not care, to do only what their arrangement required, to let them leave with their sadness, to not let her own sadness out, to stay on guard. The hotel rooms began to smell of sadness. The curtains, the sheets, the pillows, the carpeting. Drenched in sadness.

During sex the men were usually disconnected, distant, faraway minds. But what of it? Her mind, too, was far away, thinking of a new life with her brother.

But one particular afternoon she opened her eyes and looked up at a face and stiffened with fright, with self-consciousness, and she pushed him off of her and rolled to the side and buried her face in her hands. She didn't know what else to do: he had been looking at *her,* he had been doing all those intimate, sweaty things not to his own private fantasy but to her, to the person called Megumi. Her mind had been far away but his mind had been right there, between them, with them.

"Did I hurt you?" he said. "Are you okay?"

Was she okay? She wasn't sure. "I'm sorry," she said. "Let's keep going."

He wasn't like her other clients. He was unmarried, a college student, from a rich family, good looking. Smart and charming and kind. And perverted.

The next week, same thing. His mind was right there. Hers too. He paid her.

And instead of waiting for his calls, she began calling him, arranging two or three meetings a week. Sometimes four. Right there. He still paid her. Afterward they would go to a café together or a restaurant for dinner. He wasn't afraid of being seen in public with her.

But what was she to talk about at cafés and restaurants? Her other clients? How she wanted to keep her two lives separate? At first it was easy enough to just listen. Men love to talk about themselves. But after a while she was expected to contribute; she wanted to contribute. She told about her family, about how she's half Korean, about her hikikomori brother.

They'd meet in the hotel, and more and more often they'd use up the entire appointment simply talking, time flying, forgetting all about having sex. Even then he paid her.

At dinner one night he asked if she would ever go on a real date with him. "Are you running out of money?" she asked, laughing.

"I have plenty of money. But I just . . . I just love doing so many amazing things in the city, and I always do them alone and I like doing them alone but I'd much rather share them with someone else and the only person I can think of, the only person I'd really want to do any of those things with, is you."

"Don't you have any friends?" she asked.

"Of course I have friends," he said. "But nobody special."

Client, no longer. Over the next months, they saw each other often. They met after school and went to cafés and parks and gardens and restaurants. He took her shopping. They explored different neighborhoods and went to museums and baseball games and secret, hidden jazz clubs. A new, sophisticated world. Once, they went to the harbor and watched the ships being loaded and unloaded with giant, slow-moving cranes. Often, but not always, they went to hotels. One night at dinner, as he was sipping his soup, he asked her to stop seeing clients.

"If not for my clients I'd have never met you," she said.

"But now that you've met me, why do you need to see clients?"

"For the money."

"So if I paid you that much, you wouldn't see them anymore?"

"Of course."

Later that night her brother was rushed to the hospital. Three days later, in his bedroom, he slit his arms and stomach and throat.

She would've held him. Dead, alive, blood or no blood, she would've held him. He deserved to be held. He did not deserve to have his mother call the authorities and order a cleanup as though a storm had sent a tree flying through their roof. He didn't deserve to be erased for the sake of those still living. He deserved to be held.

"When my brother died," she tells Thomas, "I lost it. Is that the right way to say it? That's how it happens sometimes. You just lose it. You say, That's enough. First my brother did, then I did. I had to escape, get out of there. How could I spend even one more night in that house without losing my mind? I didn't even pack a bag. I walked out and called my friend here in New York to tell her I was on my way. The next flight wasn't until the morning so I slept in the airport. And now here I am. I thought maybe if I had told him about all the money I had been saving up, maybe then he would've changed his mind. I don't know."

"You haven't been back?"

"Not even once in three years."

"I'm sorry."

Eighteen

S HE HELPS ME CARRY the groceries home. For a moment I imagine that we are walking home together — to our own home.

I ask if she'll have enough time to get some sleep before work. "Not really. Maybe a few hours. I'll have to guzzle down coffee all day."

"Where did you learn that word?"

"*Guzzle*? I don't know. I like it because I can pronounce the two *z*s correctly. Most of my friends can't."

My street is just as lonely and quiet as before. This whole time, all these sleeping people have been dreaming. It's like the air is filled with their dreams. She asks if she can help carry the groceries upstairs. "I can manage," I say. I take the bags from her and set them on the top step, in front of the door. I put down my bags as well.

"Everything okay?" she asks.

"It happened right there," I say, pointing behind her. She spins around but there is only empty pavement.

"That spot on the road. Even now the stain doesn't wash away." My knee cracks as I sit down on the top step, facing her, facing the street. I fold my hands together. "I'm not doing this because you're here," I say. "I always do this. When I come back from my shopping in the middle of the night I set down the bags and sit here and look at that spot and think. In a way I'm sorry you have to witness it."

"You never have to feel that way about me," she says, the kind of thing people say as they fall in love, before things change.

"This is the first time we've been outside together," I say.

"Our first date."

"Is grocery shopping at three in the morning a date?"

"Sure. We were holding hands."

I lean back against the step. Morris's light is off. The concrete is rough, stones stuck together with cold gray paste. These same stones shattered my coffee cup. The coffee stain is gone. The bloodstain is still there, a black splotch. People step on it. People drive over it.

At this time of night the buses barely come and there are no cabs.

She calls a car service. While we wait she takes a pen from her purse and fishes out and unwads a wrapper or receipt of some sort, then flattens it out on her thigh and starts writing. "Just in case," she says.

"Just in case what?"

"You can call me anytime, or you can come over." She hands me the paper.

"I don't even have my own phone."

"Memorize it. The address, too. If all else fails, find the wagashi shop on Minetta. Hamamoto." I put the paper in my pocket. A few moments pass. I follow her gaze's vector straight to the stain on the pavement. "I don't know exactly what I mean by all this," she says, "but when my brother . . . I just don't want you to lose it or do anything— just come, okay? If something like that starts to happen."

"Don't worry."

"Promise?"

When the car comes she kisses me on the lips. "Thanks for coming out tonight," she says. "I feel so much better now. Because of you." She rolls down the window and waves as the car drives off.

I carry my groceries up the stairs. Five plastic bags hanging from my wrist, I open the door. It takes some time for my eyes to adjust to the bright light. How could I have been so stupid, so careless, where was my mind? Another ambush!

Silke says nothing at first, she just sits there on the sofa, staring up at me. I've seen her in the dark as I pass by her room, but when was the last time my wife saw my face? I search and search but come up blank. I feel as though I am onstage, naked.

"I didn't know you were out," she says. Her legs are folded beneath her, as they were when I'd come home late from the studio, when she'd look up from her book and smile.

She comes toward me. "Here, let me help you with that." She takes the shopping bags from my hands and goes with them to the kitchen. The most jarring thing is that she's wearing the white sundress. I'd forgotten all about that dress, but now the entire memory hits me all at once.

She puts away my groceries, clearing room in the cupboard for my dried soups and macaroni and cheese. She puts the milk and butter in the refrigerator, as though I have come home, as though she called me with a list and I have delivered.

Her face has no particular expression. She crumples the first plastic bag into a ball, throws it away, and begins to unpack the next.

My food next to hers in the cupboard looks like nonsense. "What are you doing?" I ask.

"Putting away the groceries." I tell her not to bother, that I'm going to take them back to my room anyway, but she continues to unpack. "Are you hungry," she asks, "do you want me to make you something?"

"It's three in the morning."

"Are you hungry?"

"What are you doing awake?"

She tells me she was having dreams and woke up and couldn't get back to sleep. Bad dreams? I ask, nightmares? No, she says, intense dreams. Not good or bad; just intense. "I haven't forgotten that you hate when I tell you my dreams," she says. "Don't worry, I won't bother you with the details."

Every word would be the wrong word, so I stay silent.

"Are you sure I can't make you something?"

"You don't have to cook for me."

"Then how about just a snack?"

We sit at the kitchen table under the hanging pendant lamp. Chips and salsa. The crunch echoes in my head, the tang lingers on my tongue. "They're from a new store, a tortilla factory in Brooklyn. Pretty good, don't you think?"

I nod. Here she is, within reach, all I'd have to do is extend my arm and open my hand and cup her cheek, fingers stretching into her hair.

Maybe that's Megumi's purpose, to simply get me used to having other human beings in my proximity. Why doesn't she mention Megumi's little shoes? I wait for it. I prepare a response.

Her fingers grab a chip and plow the salsa. *Crunch crunch crunch* between her teeth. A soft pulp. She swallows. A shared snack, each of us with the same taste in our mouth. Is this how it begins?

"What's going on?" I ask.

"Can't I have something to eat with you? Is that against the rules?"

"But what will it change?" I say, and I'm startled to realize that

I don't mean it as some bitter rhetorical deflection at all but as an actual genuine question to which I really want to hear her answer. I want to know whether my sitting here could really be the beginning.

"Eat your chips," she says.

For a while we do not talk. The salsa level sinks lower. The remaining chips are smaller, revealing the crumbs underneath, and the abandoned salt. She is beautiful, my wife. Whatever these years have done to her soul, her face is still beautiful. But stained with desperation.

"Maybe . . ." she starts, but then turns her head toward the window, toward the black, and in the glass I can just barely see her reflection and my arm extends and before I can change my mind my open hand settles on her cheek, soft skin, and my fingertips, yes, stretch into her hair. She does not hesitate, she places her warm hand over mine and presses hard. She does not turn toward me; she stares out the window. Perhaps she can see me in reflection.

I slide my hand out and stand up. "I should go."

"Maybe you could stay," she says without turning around. But I leave her there and go into my room and deadbolt the door.

I sit motionless on my bed and listen, but there is nothing to hear, and it is not the silence of emptiness, like the vacuum of space, the silence of nothing to say, no common point, of searching for words; it is the silence of drowning, of overflowing fullness. It is the silence of too much to say and nowhere to begin.

I pull aside the window shade but Megumi is not down there. She has not come back. She is somewhere else. It would be so easy, a fresh start, a woman I have not yet wronged.

Finally there is a sound, and it is a familiar one: Silke's sobs. Quiet at first, she spends tremendous effort holding them back. She struggles. They grow louder. I wait for her to stop, a long time, but she does not stop. The stain is my fault. I can't bear it, I go back out.

"What do you mean, Maybe I could stay?" I say. She is as she was, sitting at the table, facing the window. She wipes her tears. She tries to compose herself.

"Just for a night," she says. She turns to me. How must I look to her? I am a stranger. Or maybe she looks at my body and face and sees only memories. "I don't know if every day you're dying to come out and be with me but every day something holds you back, or if you're happy as a clam in there and have no intention of coming out, or if you're about to run off with her. I don't know anything. And my imagination . . . I get nothing from you, so I make things up. I'm going crazy out here."

She takes my hand. So different from Megumi's hands. Larger, stiffer.

"See," she says, "it's still you, still your hands and mine, still us. We're right here." And warmer. Warmer than Megumi's. "Maybe you could show me something, progress, that you're trying."

So we sit on the sofa. I'm not sure how to hold my body on the contraption, it's been so long. She keeps her distance, at the opposite end, arm against the rest, angled away. We face forward.

"What am I supposed to do?" I ask.

"Don't be like that," she says. I'm not sure if her meaning is limited to my comment or extended to encompass my entire life. *Don't be like that.* Yes, darling, I wish I weren't like that, I wish I could be like something else, someone else, everyone else.

"Maybe there's no solution," she says. "Maybe there's no . . . maybe you just pretend and pretend, little by little, until it's real." She scoots closer. She tells me that problems don't always get solved, but that we go on, that we don't need to put our lives on hold over every little thing.

"You think of him as a little—"

"Stop," she says. If we want to be together again, she says, if I want to be out of my room and happy again (she carefully avoids the word *normal*), then maybe all I have to do is pretend, all I have to do is act like someone who is (again she avoids it) not living in his room. "It doesn't have to be real, at first," she says. "You can just pretend. Like you are now."

And enough pretending will make it real. Or maybe everything is in some way pretending.

She says she's sick of talking about it. "When you're out here, we'll just live our lives as we otherwise would, and we won't try to solve anything. Solving things gets so exhausting, don't you think?"

"So," I say, "what would we be doing now, at three forty-three in the morning?"

A late-night movie is flickering against our faces. She has moved closer but does not touch me. When we used to watch movies she would place her head on my lap. The wooden coffee table at my feet: it was hers and then became ours, after we threw mine to the curb. I rest my feet upon it, like I used to, and actually until now I had forgotten that habit, that I used to sit here with my feet out, watching television. How deep I've sunk. And there, on the nearest corner, is a notch, a hacked-out chunk, where my son one day took my pocketknife and decided to teach himself how to carve ornaments into furniture. Wait until your father comes home and sees what you've done, Silke must have scolded. When I came home she said, Look what your son did. At times like those he was never her son, he was always my son. She dragged him out of his room to feel my anger. I looked at the hacked void and the naked splinters on the floor, and the still-open knife (Silke had preserved the scene) and I looked down on his guilty face. He was about to burst into tears, but—my brave boy!—he looked me in the eye and did not waver. I cracked a smile, and said, "If you can't improve the table, then don't cut into it." I patted his shaggy head and went into the bedroom to change clothes.

The wound is no longer fresh. The splinters have softened, worn smooth under waves of weeks and months and years. But I can see him there looking up at me—so guilty but unsure why—and I can imagine him finding the knife (had he seen me hide it?) and tiptoeing to see that Mom was occupied with chopping tomatoes, and I can see the glint of the blade as he opened it, his private little moment of discovery, and the joy in his eyes, the pure flowing life as the blade bit the wood. Was he surprised how easily the table yielded to his will? Was it his first taste of power? He had no wish to destroy, to merely hack and slice; no malice, no base mutilation. He was a creator: he had a plan, he had something in mind for that table. How could I be angry?

My life was not empty, as so many are, filled only with regret; it was not a sad life of wasted opportunity. My life was full and perfect. I had exactly the life I wanted; I had not squandered my talents or my intellect or even my love. And that could be the problem. The wasted life, we all think it's a shame, but what about the full life, what about the full life that can never be full enough, the life full by every measure but time?

I can barely pay attention to the movie. Sitting on the sofa like we used to, I should be saying to myself, Look how far I've come! I should be proud. And happy. Whatever we had is alive, a flicker at least. But something feels false. Undeserved. How could I have forgotten about her simple white sundress when she used to wear it nearly every night after work? "More comfy than sweats," she used to say. What else have I forgotten and how many thousand more little pieces will we have to reconstruct? A blind couple putting together a giant jigsaw puzzle, we finally found two pieces that fit together, a small triumph, but it does not solve anything. And it's nothing next to what remains. No doubt Silke feels it, too. A little hope shows how little hope there is. It's crushing.

I stand up. "I'm sorry," I say, but I'm not sure my voice matches my meaning, so I say it again. "I'm sorry." I go to my room and lock the door.

I bought the sundress for her during our first road trip together, the overnight kind, where compatibility or incompatibility is laid bare. Do we rent a sporty convertible or sober compact? Back roads or freeway? Air-conditioning or wind? Not to mention the whole issue of radio stations. Stay on course or go see what TENNYSOHN'S FAMILY FARM—FRESH PRODUCE, EGGS AND CIDER: NEXT EXIT is all about? The ability to control one's reaction to the other person's navigation errors and the resulting confusion, including but not limited to the ability to resist pointing out how easily avoidable the navigation error was in the first place, if only that person would pay attention to the real out-the-window world and its signs instead of blindly relying on the GPS. Rest stop's fast food, trucker's greasy spoon, or pack a cooler? Big hotel with all the trimmings or one of those oceanside cottages?

The faint smell of smoke.

We held hands at the top of the dunes. To the north, the lifeguard tower kept watch over the umbrellaed throngs; to the south, nobody, nothing but sand and waves. We didn't need to say even one word. The empty stretch of beach pulled us both. I wasn't a good swimmer at all and had never been in the ocean, but Silke had grown up near the water and had been on the swim team in high school. I trusted her. "The sand is nicer here in the tideland," she said. We laid out our towels. When it got too hot we cooled off in the ocean. She showed me it was okay to go out deeper so the waves would slide past beneath us. We floated together. "Never turn your back on the ocean," she said. Ocean bobs thwarting our kisses. Trying to get the timing right. Giggles at my accidental snorts of salt water. Her eyelashes sticking together. Regaining my legs, emerging from the shallows and walking back onto the shore felt strangely birthlike. She gathered her water-darkened hair and wrung it out. Grains of sand stuck to the drops and stayed that way for a while. I wiggled my back into the towel to create a perfect me-shaped cradle of sand. The hypnotic sound of spume. Skin tightening as it dries. The sun heavy on my face. What may or may not have been a nap.

On the walk back to the cottage there was the cutest little shop, as she put it. We could never stay side by side in a shop or store; we always eventually wandered off on our own. I pulled the white sundress off the rack. She turned and showed me a yellow floppy-brimmed hat. A perfect match. She tried on the dress over her bikini. I bought her the hat, too, and the lady behind the counter had

Silke turn around so she could snip off the tag. She wore the dress and hat out of the store. "How'd you know that was my size?" she asked. The dress was nothing fancy. Cotton, spaghetti straps, not too long not too short, with just the right amount of frill. Her wearing it made it look prettier than it actually was.

Smoke is supposed to dissipate. Someone always takes care of it. But this smoke does not dissipate, and it is the wrong kind of smoke. I've never smelled it before but I know it's the wrong kind.

"Silke?" I say through my closed door. I wait a moment. How long has the smoke been building? It's like when the car came speeding down the road and in my head I calculated all sorts of physics and geometry, and so now I am calculating and gathering evidence to find the smoke's source, beginning with simple questions of inside or outside, this apartment or another. Knowing the source will tell me how afraid I should be.

It's true that we look for evidence that supports what we already want to believe. It takes a disciplined mind to do otherwise. So I end up wasting precious minutes trying to convince myself that the smoke is coming from somewhere other than my own apartment. In order to tell myself that I have nothing to fear. But during those precious minutes the smoke yields to the fire, erasing any doubt.

"Silke, are you okay?"

But to my calls only the fire responds, a crackle and a rip. The color, the smell, the heat of fire, all these I knew about, but the sound of fire surprises me. Fire is a living thing, eating and burning and belching. A hot wind crackling back and forth. My shirt sticks to my skin. The fire grows, fast. Black wisps through the door's slits, as though the smoke itself is trying to escape some horror out there.

A noise that could be the front door.

"Silke?"

Time after time she called my name through my door and I was mute. Now it's her turn. To ignore. To inflict. She knows the flames will find me. She has left me to fend for myself. Who could blame her?

So this is it. Just like that, no going back. My heart pounds and my left hand quivers, but I have the courage to embrace this immolation.

She'll be outside soon. I crawl to the window to get one last look at her before she runs away. She'll look so beautiful in the streetlamps.

Shadows dance across the pavement where I let my son die.

She will run away and start over. Good for her. If I had known I'd cause her so much grief I'd have never let her come near me. I am a disappointment.

Darling!

I will sit here and burn.

My flaw will die with me. I won't pass it along, and I won't kill again. And I will be released from guilt.

I am calm.

I have fought off the future.

Black clouds press down from the ceiling, a sort of upside-down flood. The words *smoke inhalation* come to mind, abstract words in a newspaper, now real. If I have one selfish prayer left, it's for smoke inhalation. I'm not sure I could stand the burning, the smell of my engulfed hair and skin and flesh. Please lord, don't make me watch myself blister and explode.

But the street is deserted. The smoke is cactus needles piercing my eyeballs, in and out, tenderizing. I squeeze them shut. It clogs my throat and soils my tongue. Somewhere out there some glass shatters.

Flames reach my door, licking upward. Still the street is empty. I bark at the door. "Silke? Silke!" Me, fine, blister and burn, but not her!

I crawl to the door, like an animal. I pull my sleeve over my palm and retract the locks and swing open the door. A concussion of heat and smoke flings me onto my ass. I stumble upright and plunge into the black billows and orange strobes. I hold my breath.

The living room window is pushed open all the way to the top, creating a square hole whose small size requires deliberate contortions to climb into, gain solid crouched footing, and leap from. My wife Silke is at the window in just such a climbing posture. Her left foot is already in the sill, her right foot on the floor. Her arms are up, both hands pinching the frame in search of an adequate grip. The curtains are long gone. The ceiling smoke doesn't wait; it finds the hole and jumps on out ahead of her. The difference is the smoke goes up. The path to the front door is clear. Her left hand has now found its grip, but the right still searches. She tries pronating it. It's awkward. Five floors is high enough, probably, considering that below there is only concrete. It'll have to do, five floors is all this place has.

You were so happy I picked out the right-sized sundress. You thought I didn't know! You thought I wasn't paying attention.

But now the dress is speckled orange with holes glowing wider as they burn. When her right hand finally gets its grip she's pretty quick about it. Right foot in the sill. She hoists her torso into the hole. Just like she used to do on the starting block at high school swim meets. She rocks backward to gain some pendular momentum. But I'm quicker. My left arm extended like a scoop, I intercept her at the waist and then finish with my right arm in a violent sideways hug, and the amount of force I need to be absolutely certain that I get her out of the window's hole via the proper direction gives me incredible inertia and we both go crashing to the floor.

She says something but I can't make it out. Sirens are coming. I pull her to her feet. I support her weight. The flames race toward the door. The piano wires snap, one by one.

Nineteen

"THOMAS?" SHE SAYS, AND her eyes light up, but then she looks over my shoulder at my wife. Perhaps she smells the smoke.

"I have nowhere else to go."

I sit Silke down on the sofa. Megumi wears only striped panties and a thin cotton tanktop, nearly transparent, but my wife seems not to notice. She stares straight ahead.

"Sorry to wake you."

"I was reading," she says. "I think she should lie down." She walks my wife to the sofa and cradles her head as she guides it to the pillow. She asks what she needs, but there is no answer. She goes to the bathroom and comes back with a blue plastic bowl of water and small towels. She kneels on the floor and dabs Silke's forehead with a wet towel, then her cheeks, clearing away the soot and grime. "Are you cold?" she asks. My wife's only response is to look into Megumi's eyes, then mine. Megumi gets some clothes from a drawer, sweatpants and a large hooded sweatshirt, a man's sweatshirt. "Thomas," she says, "help me."

It's the first time I've seen my wife naked in over three years. Megumi pulls the sweatpants up to her waist, and I straighten her arms and pull the sweatshirt over her head, down to her waist. Megumi covers her with a blanket and says, "Maybe she should go to the hospital."

"I don't need to go to the hospital," Silke says.

It won't be long before the sun rises. The last hours have been such motion, actions and reactions, my life flipped in an instant, no going back. What of my room? Charred by now, firefighters plodding through the mess, hacking away at blackened lumber and plaster with sharp tools perfectly suited. Surges run through me, impulses, jerks, shocking my organs awake, my skin barely able to contain them, stretching then going slack as the impulses search for a weak spot, some place to release the pressure. My body finally again performing the functions for which it was made: lifting and traveling and caring. Responding to my commands. Yes sir, we'll tackle her, sir, we'll lift her off the floor and carry her down the stairs. My body is excited again, atoms and cells crashing into one another, reorganizing, roused from slumber and anxious for the next assignment, wondering if this action is the new state of things.

Her breathing is steady and slow, her sleeping sound. Had I left my room a moment later she would not be here. Because of me she is still here, but I don't know if I have saved her life or once again ruined it.

The surges inside me wear themselves out. They fade. I grow tired. Megumi pulls some bedding off the shelf and spreads it over the floor. "It's a futon," she says. "We have no choice." Under the blankets she keeps her distance but reaches out for my hand. She strokes my fingers. My wife coughs, clipped hacks, soot stuck to her throat. The surges are silent now. I sleep.

In the morning Megumi is already awake, quietly making breakfast. I go the bathroom and look into the mirror. My eyes dart away. I wash my hands. I brush my teeth with my finger. I brush and spit and lick the inside of my mouth. I still taste smoke. I brush again, and then again. I spit out all the smoke. It slides down the drain. I shower. The hot water stings my skin. I wash the smoke out of my hair.

"Don't worry about the futon," she says from the counter, shaking her head, but I continue folding the futon as best as I can, and I place it on the shelf. I join her at the counter. She gives me an orange to peel.

Silke coughs again. I go to her. Behind those shut eyes, restless dreams trying to work out if she's alive or dead.

She wakes. The two of us hover over her. I take her hand. "How are you?" I ask. Megumi goes to the counter and returns with a tray of rice, soup, a peeled orange, and a glass of water. I ask my wife if she can sit up. "I'm fine," she says.

She swallows the entire glass of water before coming up for air. She looks down at her new clothes.

———————

"I'll be back after my shift," Megumi says as she leaves. "Call if you need anything. There's an extra set of keys on the hook." She closes the door.

And so we are alone in her apartment, together in her room. The smell here is probably new to my wife, and strange and dark, the scent that has lingered in my room.

She eats all her breakfast, even the orange. I take the tray back to the counter and wash the dishes.

"Do you want a shower?"

"My head hurts," she says.

"Some Tylenol?" She nods. "Is it just your head?"

"I don't know yet."

I bring her another glass of water. She swallows the pills. "Megumi is so kind," she says.

While she is in the shower I go to the window—it's open a crack—and look outside at an apple tree. In autumn you could probably reach out and grab an apple.

She finally comes out, her hair damp. "Are you okay?" I ask. She gives me the look I deserve, yet I persist: "Do you want to talk?"

"Suddenly after three years you want to talk." Her voice spits more than rebuke. She's protecting us both. Where would we start? Maybe she would ask me why I bothered stopping her. Talking about what happened would only lead to miscommunication, misunderstanding.

"Where are you going?" I ask.

"To work."

"Dressed like that, in Megumi's clothes?"

"I'll buy something along the way."

"Are you sure it's a good idea to go to work?"

"At this point," she says, "we're all out of good ideas, don't you think? I might as well go to work."

"Well, wait a minute." I try hugging her. She is stiff, unyielding. I have overstepped some boundary. I release her but stay standing close. "It's just that I'm scared to let you leave."

"You mean you are scared to be alone, or you are scared for *me* to be alone?" Right to the heart of it, as always. I have no answer; I honestly don't know.

"It just seems wrong to be apart right now," I say.

"Wrong to be apart. Look, I know what you're getting at. Last night it all came over me at once and it felt so hopeless and . . . I never seriously thought about doing anything so drastic before." Her face does not contradict her words, and I make sure my own face displays credulity. The situation demands it. She continues. "I'm just glad, I thank god that it didn't spread, that nobody was—"

"You think they bought our story?"

"There's nothing to buy or not buy."

"A kitchen fire that got out of hand."

"That's exactly what it was." Her eyes are dead level. Not even a blink.

"They said we could take a look starting this afternoon."

"There won't be much left."

"Maybe we could go together."

"I told you, I'm going to get some clothes and then I have to go to work."

"Are you sure that's a good idea?"

Taking deep breaths and ever so slowly and loudly exhaling is a surly way to highlight the very frustration that one is purporting to suppress, but Silke was always able to pull it off in a completely natural, disarming way, as though it were something she was totally unconscious of. She does it again now. Another thing about her I had forgotten. "We can't undo last night, or any of it," she says. "And you want some sort of answer, something definitive, but you want it just so you can feel at ease and don't have to pace back and forth in uncertainty. So you don't have to suffer. And it's not that I want you to suffer, but that's just not how this works. I don't have any answers, not yet. And if you're honest, you don't either."

"So then now what?"

"Now I go to work. Just like I have been. And now you stay here and wait. Like I have."

Twenty

I WANDER MEGUMI'S APARTMENT. Just like Silke said I would. Dissipating energy and uncertainty. I don't hate it when she's right; I hate it when I should've known earlier, so I could have spared us both from her having to point it all out to me. The clock hands in the kitchen say nine thirty, plus a few seconds. The day ahead seems endless. When did that change? I used to never feel the future; I could sit idle in my room all day, perfectly calm with no sense of anything slipping away. But now the future screams for attention. An anxious mood envelops me.

Megumi's extra keys are hanging on the hook. Silke did not take them. When the fire started, my own keys and wallet were still in my pocket from shopping with Megumi. A small bit of luck.

I hail a cab. The lurch and sway is a little too much. I open the window and position my face for the right amount of air. The weather has turned. Winter, finally over.

From the outside there isn't much to see, except that some of our windows have been replaced with sheets of particleboard. The window from which my wife nearly leaped is not boarded over. The square hole is still there. It takes all my strength and willpower to avoid tracing the likely trajectory with my eyes.

The rest of the building seems fine. The street is as usual. I look at Morris's windows, but they reveal nothing. If he shows his face, I am ready.

The staircase harbors the smell of smoke but not as strong as I imagined. Nature gets right to the business of moving on. It does not dwell.

A single boot print on the door. Next to the knob. That's all it took for them to get in. The door is ajar.

Two men in heavy-looking parkas are standing in the living room with their hands on their hips and staring up at a scorched spot on the ceiling. "Yeah I don't think so either," the bigger one says. When they become aware of my presence, the smaller one asks if he can help me, a question that sounds oddly funny to me.

"It's my place," I say.

"You're the owner?"

"I mean I live here. I rented."

"You don't live here no more." They look at me the same way they did the spot on the ceiling. Something to inspect. "It says here you refused medical treatment." Not an accusation, exactly, but nor is it casual conversation.

"We were fine," I answer. "We are fine."

"Permits," the smaller one says. "That's going to be the pain in your ass. The permits."

"But it says there were only two of you. Where's the third occupant?"

"It's not that the damage is all that bad," the small one continues, "but all these walls got to come down and get replaced, so that's electrical, gas, the whole shit. This one's load-bearing over the staircase. Securing the permits is going to be a nightmare. And then Housing will take a look at the pipes and they're probably old and out of code, so that'll all have to get replaced."

"Third?"

"We just want to be sure we account for everyone."

"Not just your unit but probably the whole building might need new pipes. If the fire doesn't kill you, the reconstruction will. Be glad you're just renting. We're talking a year. At least." The smaller one then picks up two cups of Dunkin' Donuts coffee that have been perched on what used to be the sofa, which itself had at some point been flipped over and pushed askew and now smells damp and musty. He keeps one cup for himself and hands the other to his partner. He heads into the kitchen. The reflective block lettering on their parkas indicates they belong to the fire department. Beneath they are presumably wearing badges.

"It's just my wife and me."

"Right. You, your wife, and someone in the smaller bedroom. Looks like it was a woman's room." His eyes are eager and suspicious.

I suddenly wonder if this is the can-be-used-against-me type of conversation. If I have rights. "That was my wife's room. We were having a sort of . . ." But I don't know what the word is.

He sips his coffee and takes a quick glance down the hall. "So only two people lived here. You and your wife."

"Correct."

"And was anyone else here at the time of the fire?"

"No, just us."

His eyes turn indifferent. He looks strangely disappointed. "When the fire started you were where."

"In my room. Sleeping."

"Follow me," he says. At first my feet feel cold, but it turns out they are wet. I don't remember stepping in anything wet, but I must've. He picks up a burnt scrap of something. "Now I'm guessing that wife of yours thought these curtains hanging in the window here were real pretty. And they were. Right up until the point where they caught fire and started what you got here which is your classic kitchen fire. They get out of hand real quick. Was she in the habit of leaving the kitchen while she was cooking?"

"No, no, she—"

"You know how many times I've heard that? And yet here we are. And look at this—a smoke detector with no battery. You're cooking one night, the damn thing goes off, it's annoying, you take out the battery. Right?"

The smaller one says, "It's *supposed* to be annoying."

Even so, their admonishments are rote and without conviction now that there is no third person, no death, nothing to get to the bottom of. Professionally, a humdrum case.

"Show me where you kept the fire extinguisher. That's right. There wasn't one." He finishes his coffee and surveys the scene. The charred walls, the soggy ash and pulp covering the floor. "You got to have a fire extinguisher. This whole thing could've been prevented."

So true!

"Mind if I look around?" I ask.

"Knock yourself out."

The stacks of boxes in what used to be my room are burnt or wet or both. Inside, the photographs and negatives are all warped and blistered and scorched. The television is on its side on the floor. The mirror where Megumi shaved my beard is covered in soot. I want to write something in it but I don't know what. The shampoo bottle has melted into an amusing shape. These things are no longer mine or anyone else's. They simply exist as objects to be carted off.

One photo on my dresser survived, sort of, the one of me as a boy pointing at the river. I try popping it out of its frame but it is fused with the glass. When I pull, it rips. Destroyed. I take one last look at myself as a boy.

There is only one more thing to check. The most important thing. In the bottom of the middle dresser drawer. The clothes are a little damp. I lift them up and my brown pocket-size notebook is sitting there obediently. Unscathed.

I wish I could ask them exactly how the curtains ignited, without attracting the wrong kind of attention. She was not, I think, cooking. Maybe I should just take my cues from them. If they don't feel the need to investigate further, neither should I. They've seen this before. They know what is provable and what is not. What makes the difference and what does not.

Twenty-one

WHEN MEGUMI RETURNS FROM work Thomas is sleeping on the sofa. He does not snore. She sets the UNIQLO bag on the floor and the groceries on the counter.

She rinses a fresh batch of rice for dinner. Enough for three. Her cooking is a skill-in-waiting, learned from her mother as preparation for a future that has not yet come. It's nice to finally cook for someone. She mixes the miso sauce and gets the *hamachi* marinating. She tries to do it quietly even though all she really wants is for him to wake up. Scallions are next, rinsed and sliced. Growing up, she never thought it strange that her mother cooked only Japanese food, and not until she came to New York and met a lot of Koreans did she see how proud they are of their food (and how it shapes their very identities) and wonder what conflicts must've boiled within her mother.

For the moment her new brother has a Korean name. That will have to be addressed. A Japanese alias—official or otherwise— makes everything easier, no question, but at what cost?

He wakes. "Rise and shine, sleepyhead."

"I passed out," he says, righting himself.

"You poor thing. Look inside the UNIQLO bag. I bought you and Silke some fresh clothes. Just simple stuff until you get your own. Where is she?"

"She left. She went to work."

"Is she coming back?"

"I don't know."

"Thomas, what happened?"

"It was a freak thing," he says. "I went back there today and the fire inspectors or whoever they were, they showed me the spot in the kitchen where the curtains caught fire. It all spread from there."

"You guys are lucky to have gotten out." She wants to probe, but she does not.

The thought of showing up at his place to find it burnt and Thomas gone—as in gone—is too painful to even consider. Some instinct censors the thought before it grows beyond a flash. She wonders what part of the brain is responsible for protecting her from herself, and which part controls *that* part, and why sometimes it works and sometimes it doesn't.

"And that it didn't reach any other apartments. Maybe because we're on the top floor. The fire department got there pretty quick. Just as we got out."

Megumi joins him on the sofa. She squeezes his hands. "If something would've happened to you I don't know what I would do. How I'd handle it."

"I guess I was due some good luck."

"I think that came out wrong," she says.

"My good luck?"

"No, I mean that I don't want it to sound like if something would happen to you I'd only be concerned with myself. That it's not because of my . . . I'm not explaining it right."

"I think I understand."

"I could do it better in Japanese. It's just that when someone leaves, you suddenly feel sick. Not only because they're gone but because . . ." She stops for a moment to gather and translate her thoughts. "Because you are suddenly scared that they didn't really know how you feel, and now it's too late." She squeezes his hand tighter.

"Don't worry," he says, eyes soft, "they know."

"But do they? I wish I could tell you in Japanese. In English I only know the . . . see, I don't even know the word to describe the words. I only know the simple words. Not the big words with so much more meaning. Do I sound dumb in English? Because in Japanese I'm pretty smart."

"You're smart in English, too."

"I'm saying that when someone leaves, what makes you sick is that no matter what you said or didn't say they can't know—"

"You don't think they can feel it?" he says.

"They feel *something*. But not enough. Not the whole thing. You want to make them understand but you can't. It's like that kind of communication doesn't even exist."

His eyes become too much. She looks away. She frees his hands.

"Are you worried about her?" she asks.

"No, not really." A lie. The kind of lie that's not even meant to disguise itself as a lie. An open lie everyone involved appreciates. So now the acting begins. The complications. Face value, useless, except to conceal or pretend to conceal or make a show of not concealing. All to guard against an unfavorable outcome and lay the groundwork for a favorable one.

"Do you feel like eating?" she asks.

"I'm starving."

"Want to help me finish up? We'll make enough for your wife, just in case."

"Of course I'll help."

"Get changed first. I hope you like what I picked out for you."

He goes into the bathroom to change. When he comes out he gives her a slow spin. "How do I look?"

"I knew you'd go for the blue one. You look great."

He drizzles soy sauce over the fish. He mashes a cube of tofu. Squeezes a lemon. His cucumber slices are irregular. Some thick, some thin.

"So when do you think you'll be able to go back?" she asks.

"You're sick of me already?"

"You know what I mean." Though she could mean any number of things.

"I'm not going back." Which also could mean any number of things, some of which Megumi will not allow herself to hope for. But trying not to hope is itself a form of hope. "It's basically destroyed. It'll take, I don't know, a year or so at least to get it livable again. Probably just pay what has to be paid and let it go. I have to see what the lease says."

Leases, the law, technicalities, obligations, reimbursement. Deflections from the real topic at hand. As if this will all come down to what the lease says.

"Sounds like it was pretty bad."

"It could've been worse." He coughs. He stops slicing the cucumbers. His eyes lose their focus.

"There's nothing left?"

"Not really." He answers her questions with an overblown nonchalance so as not to seem evasive, which comes off as somewhat evasive. Then again it could be that the shock of it has not worn off. She can't expect him to be chatty about it. He probably still smells smoke in his nostrils. It's a good sign, though, that he's here at all, that he's able to answer her questions and live in a place other than his room. To ask for kindness, accept it, return it. All good signs. Megumi can't discount her own role in it.

He sets the table. "The chopsticks should go across," she says, "not up and down." He tries again. "No. Japanese do it like this. In front of the plate. More elegant, don't you think?"

They eat. "How do you like it?" she asks.

"It's delicious. Simple. Clean flavors."

"The rice is Japanese rice. I made it special."

"What's the difference?"

She doesn't know how to interpret his tone. "This rice was grown in Japan. It's expensive here and hard to find."

"I've seen Japanese rice in the store."

"No. The brand is Japanese but it was all grown in California."

"What's the difference?"

Again. "See how each little grain is the perfect shape? And rounder? California rice is too skinny and brittle. It breaks in the bag. And there isn't much flavor. I made this Japanese rice special for you."

The fire doesn't add up. There are gaps. Something is missing.

The hard part is not asking, because she knows she'll never get the complete answer anyway. A small form of withdrawal. Secrets that will never come out.

After dinner he cleans the dishes. "I insist," he says. His mind seems far away.

"What's this notebook?" she says with a gesture toward the sofa's side table.

He finishes the dishes and sits next to her on the sofa. "Open it."

A random page. Black ink. In the center, a small sketch, a long oval. Below the oval, in meticulous printing, the words *November or December 2007, Right Bicep, Basement.* On the facing page, another sketch, this one more of a short, bumpy line. *February 1987. Right Thumb. Mrs. Marshall's Car.*

"I don't get it."

"Look at my right arm. Higher. To the left. See it?"

"Oh!" She looks back and forth between the sketch and the scar on his right bicep.

"Feel it." She runs her finger over the hard oval, like something died beneath his skin. "It's a catalog of all my scars."

"Thomas . . ."

"There wasn't much to do. I stared at myself. I could spend all day staring at myself. And I started noticing all these little scars, hundreds and hundreds."

She explores the catalog. "Some don't have labels."

"I don't remember them all. First I just found each one and sketched. Then I tried remembering how I got it, what injured me. Some were obvious. Some I remembered my parents telling me about. There are burns, cuts, acne, surgeries, injections, bites. But some I just couldn't remember. I'd concentrate all day on one scar, trying to reconstruct my life, but I came up blank. My life through scars. But so much is missing, empty, gone. The scar is proof that something happened, but I have no idea what it is. I've forgotten most of my life."

She touches his scar again. Smoother than the rest of his skin. "It's weird," she says. "It's all healed, but it's not the same as before. So if it's not the same, is it really healed?" She kisses it. "Tell me what happened."

"I was down in the basement digging through a pile of stuff for my son's sled. No school that day, so much snow. I pulled out the sled and on my way to the stairs a mouse ran over my foot. I had to dodge to avoid stepping on it with my other foot, and I dodged right into a metal rod that was sticking out of a shelf. Punctured my arm."

"Was there blood?"

"A bunch. My son laughed and laughed. Made fun of me for being afraid of a mouse."

"And this one? Right thumb?"

"Sixth grade. It was Jamie's mom's turn to drive us home from basketball practice. We loaded into the station wagon. The windows steamed up. We were still sweaty from practice. She pulled into my driveway. It was dark by then. I got out, said good-bye, closed the door, but when I went toward the house my thumb stayed behind. It was stuck in the car door. With my other hand I had to lift the handle and open the door and pull out my thumb. I didn't feel a thing, isn't that strange? But when I got inside and turned on the light my hand was covered in blood. Wouldn't stop. Had to go to the hospital. Four stitches and a splint. I had broken it in two places. I was out for the season."

"Did the team lose because you weren't there?"

"They probably won more games without me. I wasn't any good."

"Did you ride an ambulance to the hospital?"

"My dad drove me. It was so cool to watch him run through the stop signs and flash his brights and drive faster than everyone. I forgot I was bleeding."

She opens to another page. "This one looks like a good one. Show me." He twists his forearm. Three circles next to each other, the middle one bigger than the others. She touches the scars. "But you don't remember how you got them?"

"I've tried, but I have no idea. What could that shape possibly be?"

"Maybe a bite?"

"Something with three teeth?"

She skips ahead a few pages. "Wow, show me this one!" She holds up the sketch.

"That one? That was so long ago. I don't even remember the year. I was in grade school. Maybe kindergarten." He pulls up the leg of his new jeans, but it won't go high enough.

"Take them off. I want to see."

He takes off his jeans.

She grabs his calf and pinches for a better look. "It's like a huge hole," she says.

"You're probably too young. Or maybe it was different in Japan. But when I was a kid soda came in bottles, glass bottles, in six-packs with a handle."

"Like beer."

"Exactly."

"I was grocery shopping with my dad."

"Your mom was already passed away?"

"She was still here. We were having a summer barbeque. Mom sent us out to pick up some last-minute things. Dad always had little jobs for me, and that day my job was to carry the six-pack of soda. The bottles were green. I think it was 7UP. The cardboard handle cut into my hand, but I was strong, up and down the aisle."

She strokes his leg as he talks. This is the same guy—isn't it?— who a few months ago wouldn't acknowledge her through the door, the same guy who shouted at her to go away, who pushed back her origami penguin. His frozen insides are thawing, and she is the heat source, she knows it. Not his wife. Her. If it weren't for her, where would he be? And when she makes it all the way, when his core, too, is completely thawed, where will he go?

She sees him as a little boy helping his father with the soda. Smart father: it's hard for a kid to run off to the candy aisle when he's lugging around a case of soda. Thomas must have felt so important, helping his father that way.

"Even though they were heavy, I refused to set the bottles down. I wanted to prove I could do it. I didn't need a break. But then, in the pasta aisle, there was a huge crash and I felt my legs go wet. Green glass all over the floor, and clear, bubbly soda spreading wild. I didn't understand. The handle was still in my hand. I hadn't dropped it, but two of the bottles were missing. They had fallen through the bottom of the case. I lifted it to show my father I hadn't dropped it. I was afraid of getting in trouble for making a mess in the store, but Dad didn't even look at the bottles, he was looking at my leg. A huge shard of green glass, a missile, was sticking out my leg. Half in, half out. Blood was streaming into my shoe. I wasn't wearing socks. The blood was sticky. I pulled out the glass. I don't know why but I put the glass in my pocket. There was a commotion. They took me to a back room and bandaged me. White gauze."

"It's so big. You should've gotten stitches."

"I thought I'd get in trouble for wasting soda and making a mess in the store, but my dad didn't say anything."

"Do you still have the glass?"

"It was in my room somewhere. Probably melted."

She turns the page. "What about this one?"

"Let's stop."

"Just one more. It's so interesting."

"Okay," he says, "let's do one more."

She finds a scar marked *April 2000. Central Park.* "This one."

"Nope," he says. "That one's a secret."

"Tell me."

"It's really embarrassing. Too embarrassing."

"Come on."

"Maybe tomorrow. If you're good."

"Okay I'll be good but then you have to tell me."

"I'll think about it."

"Promise."

"I promise to think about it."

She sets the notebook back down on the side table. "Only the notebook survived? That's all you brought back?"

"Pretty much. It's all I really wanted."

"It's the coolest thing I've ever seen. So precious. But didn't it hurt to see all your other things destroyed?"

"I didn't feel as much as I thought I would," he says. "Like when you come home from a long vacation and you see all your stuff again and it's all right where you left it and you wonder how you lasted so long without it but then you realize you lasted just fine and you don't really need any of it."

"Except for the notebook."

" 'My life through scars.' "

"You should write that on the cover. It needs a title."

She ignores the tension lurking below his happy façade. She'll take the happiness for as long as she can get it.

Later she readies the futon. Silke does not come back. Thomas and Megumi lie together in the darkness.

Neither of them can sleep. Their thoughts race and collide. They toss and bump into each other, struggling to find the right position. She touches him. He responds. He accepts. While he is inside her there are no thoughts. There is peace, relaxation. When it is over—like an exhale—they finally fall asleep.

Her brother walks out of his room, smiling, with a tray. He sets it in front of her.

"Sorry to keep you waiting," he says, "but for you it had to be perfect."

She tries to speak, but she cannot.

From through the open window a white petal floats in and lands in her soup.

"What luck!" her brother says.

The petal is nearly transparent, soaking up the soup.

She focuses all her energy toward her mouth, but it is no use. She is mute. Her thoughts and questions, trapped.

Next to the river she spots a turtle, trying to camouflage itself among the wet rocks, hiding deep inside its shell.

She knock knock knocks on the shell.

Big white squid, splayed open wide and hanging along a line to dry in the sun. She is so hungry.

She begins to perspire uncontrollably in the heat, and an unseen hand blots the sweat from her skin.

But she has nothing to drink.

She is so thirsty.

She wakes up and goes to the kitchen. There is a candy bar in the refrigerator. She keeps it where an American would put the butter. A grid of chocolate. She breaks off a square. She waits at the window. The breeze floats in. She allows the chocolate to melt on her tongue before swallowing.

In the morning she makes breakfast. She opens the window a little more. She needs fresh air. Spring is here. She doesn't eat much. As she puts on her jeans, he wakes up. "I left you some breakfast. And I made some extra rice for your lunch. Don't worry about dinner, I'll make it for you. The keys are on the hook."

"Is it the fancy Japanese rice?"

"Of course."

"You're spoiling me."

She kisses him on the way out. His lips are warm, but leaden.

She assumes Silke would contact Hamamoto, but Hamamoto goes about her business, coming down from her office from time to time to check on the shop, then going back upstairs.

Her father calls but she ignores it. She listens to the voicemail. It's her brother's little voice. *Noona, when are you coming home?* She listens to the message three more times. After that there's no need: his voice rings all day in her head, in her bones.

When she returns home the table is already set. The chopsticks are perfect. Thomas is in the kitchen, mixing something in a small bowl. He turns but he doesn't stop mixing. "How was work? Hungry? It's almost ready."

"It smells amazing, it smells Japanese. Is it?"

"I tried to make it like you do," he says with a smile. "Sit. Let's eat."

Broiled *saba* marinated in miso. Green beans with black sesame. Potato salad. "The rice is very special rice from Japan," he says, laughing.

"Thomas. How did you learn to make Japanese potato salad? I'm shocked."

"Don't say anything till you try it. I have no idea if I got it right. I found all the recipes online and I walked all the way to Sunrise Mart to get the ingredients. Can you believe that?"

"It's incredible." She takes a bite of the potato salad. "I don't know what to say, it's perfect." Only a slight exaggeration.

"Really? It's so different from any other potato salad. I wasn't sure I got the flavor right."

"Next time I'll tell you my dad's secret ingredients. You'll go crazy for it." She's giddy. Apart from her parents, nobody's ever cooked for her. Her past boyfriends couldn't even manage a ham sandwich. A Korean word comes to her. *Kamdongiya.* Touching, tender, affecting, poignant. This meal: kamdongiya.

While she cleans the dishes, he sits on the sofa. "I still can't believe you made all this. I had no idea you could cook." What other secrets, what other gems, are waiting to be discovered?

She finally gives in to her hope. She can see the two of them together, like this, night after night. Her brother and her family, they could wait a little longer, or maybe he'd want to try living in Japan. It's not a crazy thought. He could do his photography there. Every season they could spend a weekend in Hakone and stay at the same onsen and watch how the trees and birds and sounds and everything changes throughout the year. On the train back to Tokyo they could split a beer and bento. She could teach him a little of the language. There'd be no end to what she could show him. Tiny hidden *izakayas.* Yoyogi Park spiders. Walking around Jingumae, holding hands. Her parents would love him. He'd have to learn to bow. Cherry blossoms in spring. She bets she could even get the man who once never came out of his room to one day sing karaoke. Well maybe not in a bar, but at least in a private karaoke room. They could sing to each other. She can't sing much either. It doesn't matter. In summer, drinks at skyscraper bars high above the bustle and heat. He'd be so inspired there. So would she. Maybe Hamamoto could use her contacts to help her open up her own wagashi shop. Someplace small and special. He could take the pictures. Baseball, obviously, the Giants at the Tokyo Dome or maybe the Swallows at Meiji Jingu. In autumn, they'd share a big simmering pot of *nikujaga*. There is a whole district in Tokyo that is nothing but block after block of camera shops. Day trips to old country villages, where the food is best. The gray beach in winter, all to themselves.

"Look," Thomas says. "It's like the one you slid under my door." He picks the origami penguin up off the shelf next to the television. "Remember?"

"Actually," Megumi says, "that *is* the one I slid under your door. The one you pushed back."

"You kept it." He stands the penguin in the palm of his hand. "I was such a jerk."

"You've come so far."

He places the penguin back on the shelf exactly as he found it. "I never imagined I'd have such a reaction to you. I didn't see it coming. Back then I just wanted you to go away. I thought you were going to try to fix me."

"I wasn't. But you can't shut out the world forever."

"It never felt like I was shutting out the world. More like my world had simply gotten smaller. Like if you're here in New York you don't spend your days obsessing over what's going on in Istanbul or feeling bad that you're not keeping up with the news in Boulder or Sri Lanka. It doesn't feel as if you're missing anything. My room was world enough."

She knows the thing to do is to ask, What about your wife. But she does not.

"And I was your pest," she says.

"You were. You kept coming."

"I promised myself I would visit you only once. To get everyone off my back. I was going to make up some excuse."

"Then why did you keep coming?"

"Why did you open the door?"

They laugh. The moment hovers.

"You burrowed pretty deep," he says.

The doorbell rings. Megumi's heart leaps. Like a defendant when the jury returns, it's time to stand up and hear the verdict. She suddenly realizes that adrenaline and trembling and sweat and syncopated breathing and a concussive heartbeat are not how the body shows fear but how it purges fear. But there isn't enough adrenaline, her heart can't beat fast enough, her lungs can only expel so much, her muscles, too, have a limit to their twitch. Thomas grabs her hand. Skin suddenly moist. Whose skin? Both of theirs? A far-off moment, suddenly here. All too suddenly. And yet she wants to know the outcome faster, right away, to somehow know before she learns. It's the waiting. The struggle to keep composed no matter what. She prepares all sorts of responses, depending. She should have started preparing sooner. It's too late now. Caught up in her own delusion. But what did any of them expect? Like he said, she burrowed deep. She had to. Too much was at stake. The beach in winter, all to themselves, she can see it. Some delusions win, some lose.

"You want me to get it?" he asks. He lets go of her hand.

"No, I'll get it."

The only way to tell if her acting is good enough, if her face is managing to hide every last one of her swelling emotions, is to gauge Silke's reaction when she opens the door. But Silke's face is perfectly warm and neutral, which could mean that Megumi's concealment is successful or that Silke is working on a concealment of her own. Megumi leads her up the stairs. The expected small talk. Concern answered with reassurance. Sticking to the script.

She wants it to be over. She wants the whole world to skip ahead an hour. It does not. It slows down. Just for her. Each minute slower than the last.

As far as Silke is concerned, there is no reason she shouldn't hug her husband in front of Megumi. And there's no way Thomas can refuse. But do they have to hold it so long? At least from this angle she can see only Silke's face, not Thomas's. Silke has one hand higher than the other. Megumi can see the pressure Silke exerts on his back. Fingers pushing. Why is the heart so impractical? In this scene Megumi has no place. But does that mean she has no place at all? Silke rubs his back now. Thomas's posture is not as stiff as Megumi had hoped. But his hands are still. He is mostly the recipient.

The hug finally ends. She listens to the conversation just closely enough to hit her cues, that's all. She has nothing to add. Any closer and she might remember the exchange. Silke's offer and Thomas's acceptance. She does not want to remember any of it.

It's never been so hard to smile. Silke says she can't thank Megumi enough for all she's done, that it's all because of Megumi. She gives Megumi a bow-wrapped Tiffany box. "Try it on, see how you like it." Silke tells Thomas to help her with the clasp, then asks for his opinion on whether Megumi looks beautiful in the necklace. Thomas answers honestly. The pain deepens.

Time stays slow even after they leave. She sits on the floor. The apartment is silent. The penguin stares at her.

Twenty-two

IN THE TAXICAB MY wife apologizes in advance for the condition of the new apartment. "I've been so busy just setting up, I haven't had any time to clean. I didn't go to work. You were right. Took some personal days. It was the second place I saw and it was available right away and I've been running around like crazy picking stuff up and accepting the deliveries and all that. I hope you like it. Probably needs a coat of paint, so maybe Saturday we can go to the store and pick out colors. If I don't have to work to catch up on what I've missed. I was thinking of pale green for the living room."

She fumbles with the new key but finally pushes open the door and flicks on the lamp. "What do you think?" she says.

There is only one bedroom. This is where she has brought me to heal. Or brought us to heal. We are downtown, on Bank Street, a world away from the old place. It's softer here, leafy. It's too expensive, but she decided it's worth it for the calm street that cuts a diagonal through the grid, for the newness, a place with no stain on the concrete outside the front door. A place to heal. That is how she sees it. She expects us to start over. Past is past, future is future. America is the land of starting over.

"The rest of the furniture arrives next week," she says.

I am careful with her. She is careful with me. We circle each other. This is strange for us both, discovering what still holds true and what is new as we face the same question. Now what?

No doubt Megumi is asking herself the same thing. But she is alone. The only sounds her own. Nobody to share her fish and soup and rice. Nobody to catch her smile. Can she feel what I feel? Does that make it better or worse?

Silke sits on the kitchen floor scrubbing a spot on the cabinet. Green elastic holds back her hair. Some strands fall to her cheek. I open the refrigerator. There is some fruit. A bottle of orange juice. Three bottles of Miller High Life. My old favorite.

The bedtime awkwardness is inevitable. She diffuses it by feigning early exhaustion and the need to wake up early for a breakfast meeting at work. That way I can decide later where I'd like to sleep, without the weight of her stare. It's touching, her concern, her sympathy, her ability to think a few moves ahead. She says goodnight. She pauses, then kisses my cheek. She keeps the bedroom door open as she sleeps or pretends to sleep.

It's hard to fall asleep on the sofa. Unfamiliar creaks and clicks. A strange smell. When sleep does come, it is blank, black, a void.

When I wake, the light in the sky is just a whisper. Too early to tell if it's cloudy or clear.

I know why she's so happy, so confident. I know how she sees what happened that night during the fire, and if I'm not sure she's right, I know she's not wrong.

On her way out the door she tells me to think about a color for the living room. "Maybe a pale blue? Pale green?" she says. "I made a set of keys for you. Go outside, okay?"

The apartment still smells like the previous occupants and their stale lives, no cigarettes, no pets, but I can smell wine sticking to the paint. Lots of wine. And perfume and sweets. Have they gone somewhere together, maybe a place with another bedroom, or have they gone their separate ways? I open all the windows as high as they will go. The screens need cleaning. A spring breeze blows in. The air is fresher down here.

I walk up to Fourteenth Street to find a cell phone store. I buy the prepaid kind, with no contract.

Megumi doesn't pick up. There are all sorts of things I want to say, but after the beep I just tell her to call me back when she gets a chance.

"How about some music?" Silke says at dinner. I take another bite of pork chop. There is no fish, there is no soup, there is no rice. There are no chopsticks. There are potatoes and there are Brussels sprouts. Fork in one hand, knife in the other. From the bedroom she brings in the little clock radio, scrolls through the static, and settles on jazz. She puts the volume up but then back down a little.

"That's the problem with digital music," I say. "The fortes are too forte and the pianos too piano. Not like real life. Not like live."

"But radio stations have compressors."

"Yes," I say, not questioning where—from which man—she learned that radio stations have compressors, "but jazz stations don't use them as much, and it's still not as good as live." Well anyway, she says, now we have some music.

I cut into the pork chop with a shining new knife. Juice spills out. Not blood. Juice. I wonder why meat has juice. I say it out loud. "Why does meat have juice?"

"It's just water," she says. "The water from inside the cells."

"Are you sure?"

"No, but aren't we made of sixty percent water?"

"Pigs too?"

The trumpet stops abruptly and the piano picks up the riff,

tentative at first as though trying on stilts for the first time, searching for balance and rhythm. The trumpet plays a soft reminder, just a few notes, a gentle nudge, and then the piano takes off again, on its own now.

I wash the dishes. She put up a mild, fleeting protest, I insisted, she put up an even flimsier counterprotest, adding an "Are you sure?" — and now she sits on the sofa thumbing through a magazine while I clean the plates and utensils and glasses, jazz at my side.

"I have some movies," she says. "Oh—and before I forget, the cable guy is coming tomorrow to hook us up. Between twelve and four. Will you be here?"

"Yes, I will be here."

The movie is funny. We laugh together. I used to love talking during movies, and the memory returns of one of our first dates, a late-night movie in a nearly empty theater. I held her hand, which she liked, but I kept talking to her and the screen, which she did not. She wriggled her hand free and dropped it uselessly on her own thigh.

The credits roll, outtakes cut back and forth, the botched lines and failed improvisations, and it's time for bed. That is what couples do; they agree on bedtime. "You first," I say, motioning to the bathroom. When she finishes splashing and spitting and flushing, I enter the bathroom and lock the door. She has left behind a trail of scents. Face wash, toothpaste, mouthwash, cream. A woman, fragrant, ready for bed. Ready for what will happen in bed. Next to her, I am dirty. I merely brush my teeth. I don't even floss.

There is no bedside lamp yet, so she lies in bed beneath the ceiling bulbs, which are way too bright. She leaves her breasts exposed. They still sit upright, gravity has not yet claimed them. Such pale, pink nipples. Smaller than Megumi's.

"I think I'll sleep on the sofa," I say in the doorway. "It's just—"

"It's okay, don't worry. I understand. No one ever said this would happen all at once."

I turn out the light, surrounding her with darkness.

The next day at about two o'clock the cable guy arrives. He does not, near as I can tell, regard me with suspicion, the way the clerk at the convenience store always regarded me. No trace of apprehension. It appears that from looking at me he cannot tell that I have spent three years in my bedroom. Even if he knew everything—if he could somehow see it on my face—he'd respond as everyone else: that it was an unavoidable accident. Nothing I could've done. It's all in my head, that's what he'd say. Get over it, he'd say. But don't you understand, I'd say, I killed him! Who's to say I won't do it again? Get over it, he'd repeat. Because that's how people distill complexity. And anyway, he'd say, you're out of your room now, aren't you? Move on.

But all he sees is a guy who just moved into a new apartment and needs his cable television and high-speed Internet installed, and all he says is, "Over there?" while pointing to the television. His boots clunk on the wood floor. He drops to his knees, over which he wears pads with an elastic backside and hard plastic frontside, and gets to work.

I try to busy myself in the kitchen, to give him his distance, space in which to work, and I make some noises from time to time, clinks and clanks that let him think I'm preoccupied and not actually watching his every move. He strips the insulation off some wire with a special tool, exposing the shiny metal line. Work. This man is performing work. The apartment he leaves will be different from the one he entered—it will have continuous entertainment streaming into it. A thrill overtakes me, like I want to get down on my knees beside him and offer my assistance. I could hand him his tools and take them back when he's finished and place them in the correct compartment in his toolbox. I could learn from him. I could watch and learn and ask questions and in time if I proved worthy he'd let me connect the wires and test the current. I, too, could work. I could be meaningful. Silke would be proud of me were I to leave every morning and mix with the world and accomplish some tasks and then return at the end of the day to share my experiences and spend time together with her.

I want to interrogate this man who uses his hands to rearrange the world, but I cannot find an opening line. How long have you been installing cable television? I want to talk like a man. I want to talk about coaxial cable and fiber optics.

When he is finished I offer him a drink. "All we have is water and orange juice." (I don't have time to consider in what sense I used the word *we*.) He opts for juice and I hand him a glass. He chugs half all at once and then wipes his mouth with the back of his hand and the back of his hand on his Dickies.

"Nice place," he says. "Just moved in?"

"A few days ago. The last place caught fire."

"Here in the city?"

"One hundred ninth Street."

"Fucking sucks, man. Lost everything?"

"Everything."

He sips the juice, a small sip this time, as though attempting to show some respect. "Well, you have a good place now. You'll build it all back up."

"Kind of small?"

"They're all kind of small around here. That's why we live in Queens. More room, a yard, my wife tries to grow tomatoes."

"Tries?"

"Actually she does all right with the tomatoes. It's the lettuce she has a problem with."

So this is how people talk. This is how two strangers learn about each other or try not to learn about each other or try to not let the other person learn about them. And I'm so good at it! How did I get so good?

"I'm going to have to head down to the basement to reset the unit connection. You need a key to get in there?" I tell him I have no idea, that I've never been down there, and I offer to go down with him. He tells me not to bother, that he'll go down alone and if he needs a key he'll come back up or ask the doorman. He is either treating me like a client (not wanting me to needlessly exert myself) or he is concerned for his safety. Humans have an instinct that strangers and basements do not mix.

When he comes back up twelve minutes later he tells me I'm all set. He turns on the television and runs through some setup menus and suddenly the first image appears, an anchor behind a news desk. He flips through the channels. All seems to be working perfectly.

After dinner Silke and I assemble the new bookcase. "Did you ever go to the doctor?" I ask.

"For what?"

"For the smoke."

"I didn't go. You?"

"No."

"We seem to be okay."

No more sobbing, no more outbursts, no more plates smashing against the walls. Just like that. What happened to her—to us—in that fire? I'm tempted to call her delusional. Silke, you're delusional. You ignore the basic facts, which are as follows. I let our son die and you hate me for it. Rather than fusing together in our moment of abject grief I selfishly retreated into my own tiny world and left you out there to fend for yourself. For reasons known only to yourself, you stayed out there, just outside my door, waiting. What hell I was going through, and what hell you were going through! I took advantage of your love, your generous heart. I bled it dry. And yet I cannot deny the urge welling up to embrace her and hold her face and kiss her lips and say, What was I thinking, hiding away like that, sitting in silence, cataloging my scars? Who was that man in his room? It wasn't me! You're all that matters!

It's a second shot at life, at everything, and I should be diving in, head first. But I have underestimated the effect of the wall, of the closed door that for so long stood between us. I have returned home from outer space, from war, and I'm not sure where I am, what the rules are. We are together again, but we don't know where to start.

With Megumi, all is new. It flows easier. There is no past, no need to reconcile who I was with who I've become. It would be easy to dismiss her as mere distraction, except for the intensity of my feelings. The intensity is real. A heart can love twice.

Two strangers in an earthquake. Trapped, they share the same black, dusty space. They nourish each other's souls and keep each other alive until at last help comes and they emerge from the rubble holding hands. But for how long? How long before the sunlight shows the truth?

It is the same with Megumi. It is the same with my wife.

"Silke," I ask, "don't you blame me?"

She doesn't take her eyes off the television. "I've told you many times I don't. I'm happy to have you back."

Twenty-three

IN THE MORNING SILKE packs a small suitcase. "It's only for a couple nights. I don't understand why everyone likes San Francisco so much," she says. "The city is boring, the conference will be boring, a bunch of stuff I already know. But so much about holding down a job is just going through the motions, don't you think? Which is better, the black skirt or the gray?" She holds them both up for my inspection. I nod toward the black. "Not too dressy?" I shake my head. "Not too sexy?" I have no idea how to answer. She laughs and packs them both. "I want you to get out of the house while I'm gone. Promise?" I nod. "Why don't you go see Megumi? I can tell you miss her. Go. Promise?"

All eyes are on me as I enter the store. I don't know how the Japanese girls know who I am, but they know.

"Thomas," she says and comes out from behind the counter. She looks so different in her work uniform. She grabs my arm and presses tight. "Is everything okay?"

I wait for her to change clothes. The Japanese girls smile at me, trying to make me feel comfortable, but I know what they are thinking.

She has her purse and jacket. "Let's go."

A coffee shop. Surrounded by people. I told her I could handle it. I insisted. She waits at the table, an old, circular bistro-style with marble top and iron base, while I place our order with the cashier. Two coffees and a large cookie on a tray. I set the tray on the table. Megumi already has the napkins. "I hope you like chocolate chip," I say. "Let's split it."

I haven't been in a room so loud in a long time. A polyphony of conversations, clinking tableware, laptop keyboards, hissing espresso machines, orders called and confirmed, newspapers folded back, laughter. Megumi breaks off a piece of the cookie.

"How's the new place?" she asks.

"Why didn't you call me back?"

"I was going to. Last night. But I didn't want to disturb you."

"You wouldn't have been disturbing anything."

The cookie gets smaller. Megumi refills her coffee. She says I look like I could use a refill, too.

"I've been sleeping on the sofa. It's not very comfortable."

"Then here, let me get you another cup."

She asks again about the new apartment and I tell her the minimum. She asks about the old place, what's going to happen to it, and I say that Silke is working on it but it's on hold while she's away for a couple of days, but that I don't want to live there again. She says she understands, that if she were me she wouldn't want to live there anymore, either.

"You know what I need?" she says. "Actually, you know what we both really need? Some time away. Some time out of the city."

"Where do you want to go?"

"I mean both of us. Together. Let's go to the onsen. Remember?"

"The one upstate."

"We don't even need to pack anything. They'll take care of us. Let's just go. Right now."

Years of stillness, and now such motion. From the train window the world rushes by. A balm of strange thoughts floods in and out, and I think of Einstein and how he'd like the way I describe my view from the train—world rushes by—since from my perspective it is perfectly reasonable to conclude that I am still and the world is moving past, the trees and the houses and the hills. But to someone eating a picnic on the hill, it looks like I'm the one moving, here then gone; appearing then disappearing. Life is relative.

Megumi sits next to me, her head on my shoulder, and she is sleeping, and it looks like we are both sitting still with the world passing us by. Life is relative but death is absolute, or so I thought. But I see now that my problem with death has always been one of perspective. I see my life and death not from my own perspective, but from the perspective of that man picnicking on the hill, and I'm jealous that he'll remain on that hill after I've passed through.

"Here," she says. From her purse she pulls my notebook of scars. "You left it at my place."

"You've been carrying it around?"

"I read every page. I know all your scars."

The train cuts through the forest. Our motion smudges the flowers into little dots and streaks of color. The world out there undulates in graceful waves of green far into the distance, an endless green ocean frozen in time. And there is also blue, and there is white, an entire world made up of three colors. But I look closer, my focus shifts from the immense sweep of it to the fine details, and I see not just three colors but thousands, millions maybe. The green of the trees is not one uniform green but a pointillism of uncountable hues, light and dark, reflecting sunlight from every possible angle, shimmering in the breeze. And the sky, too, is not just blue but has subtle gradations from the palest of pale blue to the richest, thickest blue, and the clouds are not just white but brilliant, blinding white and gray, and as they float along unseen currents, their shapes and colors morph ever so slowly and I realize I have been holding my breath.

At the end of the line we transfer to a taxicab and plunge deeper into the green waves, into the mountains. The trees split open just ahead of us and close up behind us, like we have been swallowed and are being pushed along by the forest. In the road's curves and switch-backs and climbs and descents I lose my sense of direction.

"There it is!" Megumi cries. The driver slams on the brakes and whips around the wheel, turning the car onto a narrow road, almost hidden, marked only by a cluster of bamboo, tall and modest, bowing elegantly upward, tiny leaves dancing. "That bamboo is the only sign," she says. We drive along, veering left and right with the road, until we come upon a woman, a Japanese woman in a smart black uniform standing at the side of the lonely road. The woman marks the entrance to the onsen, and as we turn into the driveway she bows.

The entrance looks like nothing, just a door of dark wood flanked by bamboo, but inside I step into an alternate reality of simple beauty, the long reception room bathed in soft amber hues and an overwhelming fragrance of wood. Encased in the black walls is crisscrossed bamboo, each piece at a slightly different angle to form a hypnotic geometry. Along both sides and at regular intervals between the bamboo geometry are floor-to-ceiling panels that glow golden from within.

The entry is silent but for the slight burbling of water. In the center of the room is a small fountain, water cascading over polished slabs of black marble, collecting in a shallow square pool. The water is so thin and clings so tightly to the slabs that it looks as though the stone is alive with shimmering skin. Megumi motions for me to remove my shoes.

From the balcony outside our room, I look across the valley at the towering, verdant mountain peaks. The smell of life rolls off the mountains, a breeze. No human sound can be heard. Megumi joins me at the railing. She touches the small of my back, gently. "Your turn," she says. "Go change clothes. I'll wait here."

Folded neatly on a side table is a set of the clothes I'm supposed to wear for the duration. Looks like a thin robe of gray cotton, with blue brushstrokes forming abstract bamboo. And sandals, intricately carved and lacquered black and gold with braided thong. I do not understand, but I change into the clothes, trying to remember how Megumi looked in her set, identical but for size.

She giggles when she sees me walk out of the bedroom. "It's not okay?" I say.

"It's okay. Come here. You're all disheveled."

"It's a robe?"

"Yukata. Bathing clothes. Not exactly a robe. You'll understand later."

She straightens my yukata, pulling it tight and crisp yet leaving it comfy.

"And this?" I say.

"An *obi*." She wraps it around my waist and ties it properly for me.

She makes tea, which we sip out on the balcony as we listen to the birds call back and forth, tree leaves rustling in the breeze.

We walk together to the baths along a narrow downhill path of stones. Along the way she describes in detail the rules and rituals of the onsen. Making a mistake would be seriously offensive, she says, and we would be asked to leave. There is a women's bath and a men's bath. We agree to meet back in our room in no more than two hours.

"Good luck," she says.

The locker room is empty, silent. I remove my yukata and obi and place them in a wicker basket. I grab two towels and step outside, into the clear air. How unreal it feels to be outside and naked. Here, already, I feel I am again who I was before.

In the steaming pool of water only one man sits. Asian, eyes closed, a white towel resting on his forehead. I sit on a stool at a faucet and fill the wooden bucket with hot water and pour it over my head and body. I pour liquid soap onto a nylon washing towel and lather and scrub every part of my body, as though my skin is covered with a layer of stubborn dry paint. The scrubbing takes a long time and I wonder if I am scrubbing my skin raw. I pour hot water over myself to rinse, then I start over, repeating the entire ritual two more times.

The heat of the bath scalds my skin, and I am light-headed. I might pass out. My blood is in shock. I breathe deeply, slowly.

Sunlight distills through the trees, glinting off the rippled water. The bath has no straight edges, its form dictated by the shape of the rocks surrounding it. The giant rocks are not just around the bath but inside it as well, three of them, their tops peeking out of the water like volcanic islands. Pungent mineral steam gives the air a prehistoric, primordial feel, and I am immersing myself in it, becoming part of it.

Just beyond the bath, surrounding it, are tall stands of bamboo. They creak in the breeze. My tears drip into the bath. They churn with the mineral water and evaporate into the breeze.

The other man who soaks in the pool pays me and my tears no attention. We are both alone, in our own worlds. I try to clear my mind.

Has there ever been such a thing as a shared experience, a shared life? Right now Megumi and I are sharing an experience: we are soaking in the onsen. We are naked. We can hear the same creaking bamboo. Were I to shout her name toward that fence, she could hear and respond. But we cannot see each other; we are in two different pools separated by a tall wooden fence.

I step out of the bath. Water falls off my skin and splatters against the stones. As Megumi instructed, I go back to a faucet and wash as I did before. I have never been so clean. My heart has taken on the pace of nature.

I slip back into the heat of the bath, a different spot this time, in the shade of some tall birch trees. I soak for a long time. The light striking the mountains has changed and is changing, subtly, slowly, no longer at full force. The sun is on its way down.

Twenty-four

THE SLIDING DOORS ARE open, the sun has dipped behind
the mountains, and cool air rolls into the room. The wind
rustles the leaves. Dinner is served in their room. They sit across
from each other at a low table made of carved wood. They don't
sit directly on the floor, but on *zaisu,* high-backed legless wooden
chairs with silk cushions.

An elaborate dinner of fifteen courses and sake is brought to their
room, course by course, over the next few hours. Megumi shows
Thomas how to admire the plates and bowls and describes the food

to him. He eats everything put before him, and drinks all the sake and asks for more.

After dinner they sit together on the balcony and have another drink. Across the valley the mountain is cloaked in black. Megumi can just barely make out the summit, but if she stares at it too long it disappears. The sake slides down her throat. "This place makes me miss home," she says. Insects chitter and *chirr*.

"I was ready," he says. "When I was finally face to face with death, I was ready. And now I'm not afraid. Not anymore."

She reaches out and holds his arm, but says nothing. From the distance comes echoing laughter. It grows louder, then fades away. "C'mon," she says, "we have to go to the onsen."

"Again?"

"While we're bathing they'll make up our futons."

The narrow path down to the onsen is cast in gentle moonlight. Strange shadows cross the stones. They walk in silence. When they reach the entrance she says, "Want to go together?"

"Into the onsen?"

"Yes."

"It's allowed?"

"There's a family bath for men and women together."

He nods.

"From the locker room one exit leads to the men's, the other to the family. I'll meet you out there."

When he comes out, she is already sitting on the wooden stool, scrubbing, covered in suds. He sits on the stool next to her and begins washing. She smiles at him but then goes back to herself; she does not stare. In the moonlight there is little to see, just random glints of bubbles and skin. From time to time she can feel his eyes upon her naked body.

She rinses off and picks a spot facing the mountain silhouette and lowers herself into the water. There is another couple in the bath, sitting side by side. The man's eyes are closed, but the woman is watching Thomas.

Thomas rinses off and walks over to Megumi. In the silver moonlight he makes no attempt at modesty. He lowers himself into the water, next to her, letting out a little grunt against the intense heat.

The birds are silent now, but a chorus of a thousand insects and animals rings out from the trees. At the far end of the onsen the little replenishing waterfall splashes. The water laps against the rocks and against her bare shoulders. Her heart beats fast.

"I used to think that people were frightened by my guilt, that their fear was what kept them away," he says, "but now I know it's much worse. Guilt isn't frightening—it's irrelevant. The world is indifferent to guilt. In the city there are so many people walking around, going about their day, indifferent to guilt, indifferent to my guilt. I guess they have enough guilt of their own, no need to deal with anyone else's. Out here it's the same. I'm up against the indifference of this vast nature. Who am I, what is my guilt next to that, next to the giant mountains and trees? These mountains see guilt and simply stare back at me as if to say, So what. My guilt has no release. My guilt is met with endless indifference, endless silence."

It's nearly midnight. The moon and its light vanish behind a solid bank of clouds. Here and there sit small lanterns, imparting a subtle wash of radiance over the water and rocks.

"I'm very tired," Thomas says. "It's hard to stay awake . . . too much sake and steam."

The futons are laid out next to each other and folded down neatly. In front of him she takes off her clothes and crawls naked into the futon. He takes off his yukata. He has an erection. He gets into the futon and passes out instantly. She reaches over and puts her hand around his erection and squeezes. She slides her other hand between her legs, full of intentions, but she, too, falls asleep. Sake and steam.

She wakes in the morning to the sound of heavy raindrops slapping against the leaves of the trees. Thomas is not in the futon. She props herself up and rubs her eyes and spots him outside on the balcony, sitting in a chair, looking out at the rain, dressed in his yukata.

"Good morning," she says as she hands him a cup of tea.

"Thank you," he says. He smiles.

She sits in the chair next to him. "There was a certain kind of tea my dad would always pull out and drink when it was raining. A certain kind of *sencha*. He said it tasted best with a steady rain, and a steady rain looked better when you drank it. This isn't quite it, but it'll do."

"It's delicious."

There is a wet chill, a cold bite to the air. The tea warms her hands and warms her insides. Clouds hang low over the valley, dissolving the mountaintops. From their perch halfway up the mountain, they are just barely underneath the cloud ceiling. If it were any lower, they would be swallowed up; their world would turn misty white.

"I never knew the sound of the rain could be so rich," he says, "so beautiful. It woke me up. I came right out here, just to watch and listen."

"We should get to the bath."

"In the rain?"

"Haven't you figured it out yet? Bathe, eat; bathe, eat. That's all we do here. And it's amazing in the rain. After drinking so much last night we both could use a good soak."

They soak together, shoulder to shoulder in the rain. The water's surface is pitted and rippled from so many raindrops. They are not alone. Two other couples, all sitting on the same side of the onsen, face out to the mist and mountains. She tilts her head back and lets the cold drops splash against her face.

During breakfast the rain stops. "The world is so small," she says, just above a whisper.

"What do you mean?" He takes a bite of rice.

"We're always looking for some sort of bigger world. Something bigger, better. Maybe this country is for me just one big bedroom, away from my family and my past. Maybe my brother withdrew to his room and you withdrew to your room and I withdrew all way across the ocean, all the way to New York. Maybe I'm just as stuck as you are. Maybe I'm hiding from the future."

"Maybe we are."

"No matter how big we try to make our world, in the end it's just ourselves. We follow ourselves around everywhere."

They bathe again after breakfast. Neither says much. The clouds burn off. Birds fly through the air. The sun is shining, but the day is not hot. When they return to their room, breakfast has been cleared from the table.

"This place is like magic," he says. "Everything happens invisibly and perfectly."

"Are you ready?"

"Ready for what."

"We're going to cut your hair." His eyes open wide as she takes out a scissors. "I had them send up a pair. You can't go back into the world with that ragged hair. They'd never take you."

"Do you know what you're doing?"

"I figured out how to shave you, right? Let's finish the job."

She sits him down on the balcony chair.

"Oh wait," she says. "I almost forgot. I got too excited to chop it off. Here, look." She pulls out from her pocket a disposable camera. "I picked it up from the gift shop."

"There's a gift shop?"

"Of course. You can buy the plates and sandals and robes and all that. We need to take before-and-after pictures." She snaps a picture before he has a chance to pose. She turns the wheel to advance the film.

"Take a better one."

"Okay," she says, "turn your head a bit." She takes the picture. "Now another one, straight on. Thomas, smile. How about one of us together." She crouches down next to him. She puts her head against his and extends her arm, pointing the camera back at their faces. "Think we got it?"

"Take another just to be sure," he says. "I might have blinked."

She smiles for the camera and asks if he's smiling. "Okay, one more. Your last moment with long hair." The shutter clicks. She sets the camera on the wooden side table. "Now let's get you to the sink and get your hair wet."

She wets his hair and drapes a thick, white towel over his shoulders, then goes back to the balcony chair and cuts his hair. She is meticulous. It takes over an hour. He sits still and looks out at the mountains rising up from the valley. She cuts in silence, concentrating. He says nothing. The breezes come and go, softly. Birds in twos and threes fly past. The air smells of soil, still moist from the morning's rain. A pile of dark hair encircles his chair.

If only the world could stay away, if only it weren't lurking out there, beyond the mountains, waiting. Waiting like those spiders in Yoyogi Park when she was a child, walking with her father. Waiting in their webs, seeing everything but doing nothing, nothing until the right moment, when some bug gets trapped. If only it were always as simple as this.

"I'm trying to give you a cool style," she says as she puts on the finishing touches. "But it's going to look sort of choppy. Uneven. Hope that's okay."

She takes the after pictures, of him alone and of the two of them together. She sits on his lap. She smiles.

"I can feel the breeze against my scalp. I feel like I could run really fast. Or fly. But how does it look?"

"Thomas! You're so handsome. See for yourself." She leads him by the hand to the mirror. He bursts out laughing.

"What is it?"

"Nothing, nothing," he says. "For a first try it's pretty good."

"I did my best."

"I know you did. I like it. No, I love it."

"Really?"

"Yes, really, I'm just laughing because I don't know who that guy is. I don't recognize him." He turns his face from side to side, slowly, checking the view at different angles and he slides his fingers through his new cropped hair. "Megumi, you've made me into a different person."

She runs her fingers through his hair. "And you, me."

Late that night, after dinner, they soak together in the mineral-clouded water. The moon is thin and sharp, and a million specks of brilliant starlight fill the sky. With a bamboo bucket she pours water over his head, warming his face. He does the same for her. It is after midnight and they are alone in the onsen. The wet rocks glimmer in the soft light of the lanterns. Their light makes the darkness darker. The bamboo creaks, as though secrets are trapped inside.

His head tilts straight back; he looks up at the stars. Under the surface of the cloudy water he finds her hand and holds it. "It seems we've both been stuck for a while," he says.

"Yes . . . I've been stuck, too."

"I wonder what's out there waiting for us."

"Only one way to find out."

"What if when she comes back, I'm not there? What if I left, what if you and—"

"I'm going back to Japan." She blurts out the words, and until now she hadn't admitted her decision, even to herself. "I wasn't sure how to tell you. My father and mother got back together . . . and I have a new little brother. He's three."

A cloud covers the moon.

"It's my real life," she says. The water laps soft and warm against her bare shoulders. Has she stung him? Was she too blunt? "They need me there. My little brother needs me."

He squeezes her hand tighter under the water. "You get older and your real life gets narrower and narrower," he says. "Sometimes you just think, Maybe . . ."

"Even if we aren't everything, that doesn't mean we're nothing."

"I wish I didn't have to let go."

For a long time there is only silence.

"I'll miss you," he says.

"Do you know my heart?" As soon as she says it she knows it doesn't sound right in English. She tries again. "Can you tell what's inside?"

"I can feel it. What about mine?"

"I can feel it, too."

"Don't forget, okay?" he says, putting his head on her shoulder.

Megumi holds out her pinky. Thomas interlocks it with his own. "Promise," she says.

That night she does not sleep. She sits on the balcony alone or she sits on the floor next to sleeping Thomas, watching his chest rise and fall, watching him turn, watching him dream.

In the morning, at the entrance to the changing rooms, he asks if he can bathe alone. The look in his eyes tells her his meaning.

"Are you sure?" she asks.

He hesitates for a moment, but then nods.

"Okay then," she says, looking into his eyes, barely able to speak, a bitter pit already forming in her throat, "see you later, Thomas."

She enters the changing room. She takes off her clothes and washes her body and she soaks underneath the creaking bamboo, and in the hot water she cries, naked, uncontrollably, her nose running, her eyes swollen nearly shut, her breathing erratic, as though she is gasping for life and breath.

This whole time together, all this time, and now this, so fast. Ripped apart! Too fast!

She buries her face in her wet hands. The other bathers pretend not to notice. They wish for her to go away. She is spoiling the tranquility. They cannot hear the rustling leaves above her sobs. But her tears will not stop falling.

She walks slowly up the narrow path to their room. Inside she finds his yukata folded neatly on the bed. His clothes are gone. Thomas, too, is gone.

Sitting atop his yukata is his notebook. On the cover he has printed the title in black ink. *My Life through Scars.* Her eyes swell and overflow.

Twenty-five

WHETHER I JUST HAPPENED to walk past the camera store or the store somehow pulled me toward it, I do not know. I stand on the sidewalk facing the front window and dozens of cameras stare back at me, like little cyclopean puppies waiting to be adopted. It is daytime, afternoon, and I am amid the swirl of people and of life. They sometimes bump into me as they pass and I do not convulse; I feel a strange energy, as though I have discovered someplace new.

One particular camera keeps staring at me, an old Hasselblad with an 8omm lens. I go inside. The man pulls it off the shelf for me. I am surprised that my hands are ready for the weight of it. They have not forgotten. They have been waiting to hold this camera again, the same kind that I used every day in my studio. My fingers know right where to go. I look down into the viewfinder. What a comfortable way to see the world.

I hand over my new credit card, with no idea if it can cover such an expensive purchase. What did Silke set as my limit? And now the clerk and the store will know my name. It's a new world.

On a bench in front of a café, in the shade of a green awning, I pull the camera out of the box and load two backs with film. My fingers do not fumble, not even a little.

I walk through my new neighborhood, and I take pictures on the street as if I am an explorer. This world, unseen before now. I focus on a cat investigating the tire of a parked car and press the shutter. The cat and I go our separate ways, we both have lives to lead, but now I have something immortal, I have a picture of that cat sniffing a tire. Already that moment, that 1/125th of a second has passed, but I'll always possess it.

The whole time in my room I felt like a photograph in Silke's wallet. She carried me around always but I remained mute and motionless. And now here I am. Human beings are meant to move.

But my walk is unbalanced, lopsided. My body is cleansed, cleaner than it's ever been, but I don't feel quite right. A huge part of me—the new me—is empty. I have gained a lot, I have regained my life, I have made my choice, but without Megumi I feel as though I am missing a vital organ. One of my lungs. One of my eyes. I'll never get it back. All I can do now is adjust. What a sad, impotent endeavor. Getting used to it: the slow, systematic destroyer of passion.

I left something else for her besides my book of scars. I hope she understands my meaning. I think she will. She found something inside me that nobody else could ever find. She has a direct channel. Kindred spirits groping in the dark for each other, blind, pure nameless feelings intertwined. Forever.

Pale blue paint. Silke was right. The first coat is drying. I sit in the center of the room on the floor eating a ham sandwich and sipping a Miller High Life. She was right.

With the camera I could work again. I could open up a small studio and begin again taking pictures of things and put those pictures in advertisements and packages and websites. Each morning my wife, Silke, could make me a pot of her coffee.

Dipping the roller in the paint, swishing it back and forth a bit, spreading the paint evenly over the wall, this is work. This is improvement. This is me saying I was here, that I have made a change. I have painted the four walls of a room. The smell of the previous residents is gone, and I open the windows to let the fresh air mix with the paint. I clean the rollers and brushes. I pull off the blue masking tape. I crumple up the vinyl drop cloth and take it downstairs to the trash.

A spring training game is on TV, Yankees and Phillies. I watch even the late innings, when the stars have showered and gone and the hopefuls work on their swings. The rhythm of baseball soothes me. Always has. Even now when I think of the day I took my son to the game I am soothed, soothed by the knowledge that I once took my son to a baseball game. I remember it. I will always remember it.

She sets down her suitcase. "Thomas, what have you done? It's beautiful."

"You," I say, "not me. You picked the color, I just covered the walls with it." She kisses me on the lips and I do not resist. She tries not to act stunned.

"And your hair!"

"Do you like it? Megumi cut it." I think of the look on her face when I left her at the onsen. I struggle to keep my expression neutral, to not betray my emotion.

"So you saw her."

"I did."

"How is she?"

"She's going back to Japan to be with her family."

We order pizza and eat on the floor in the living room, huddled around the pizza box as though it is a fire, a hearth, while watching the detectives on *Law and Order* interrogate a suspect. "I can't believe you found the perfect color and painted the living room." She opens a can of beer and we share it, alternating sips, back and forth, as we eat and watch.

We are silent until the next commercial. She takes a bite of pizza and before she swallows she says, "Maybe one day we can visit her. I've always wanted to go to Japan." Tears fill my eyes but do not fall.

"I'm beat," she says, "do you mind cleaning up?"

I turn out the kitchen light when I'm finished and I stand in the bedroom doorway. "Would you have really gone through with it?" I ask.

She lets out a breath. "It wasn't a test, or a cry for help, if that's what you mean. I've cried enough already, don't you think? I snapped. I would've really done it."

"What made you snap?"

"It doesn't matter."

"No?"

"Does it matter why, exactly, you withdrew, and why, exactly, you refused to come out for so long? I can guess pretty close, and you could try to tell me, but I'll only understand the broad strokes. Nobody can ever really understand. Your reasons are private. My reasons are private. Not because we shouldn't know, but because we can't ever really know. The more we say the less we understand." She pulls the blanket up, all the way to her neck.

"Then what makes you think everything is okay now," I ask, "and what makes you think it's going to be okay?"

"I said it wasn't a test and that's true, it wasn't. But when you came out, when you did what you did, I realized I had an answer I wasn't even looking for, and once I had it, once I knew the truth, how could I ignore it? How could I be the same?"

She stops. She expects me to say, What answer did you find? But I am cautious. I wait—I, the silhouette leaning against the doorframe.

"You could've stayed in there and died," she says. "Or you could've run right past me and out the door."

"I could never—"

"But when you pulled me out of that window I had my answer. You chose to save me and yourself and us."

"A stranger would've done the same thing."

"A stranger, maybe, and someone in love, but not someone who hates, and not someone who's indifferent. Only someone who cares enough to risk his own life."

"It'll fade. I have no shining armor."

"It isn't always going to be pretty, I know that. But at the very heart of it, when everything was stripped away but life and death, you chose me and us and life. And yourself. You took me into your arms and pulled me back. That's how I know."

"I tackled you, is what I did."

She chuckles. "I didn't see you coming. I felt you before I saw you. I felt everything. Before we even hit the floor, I knew."

She is right. The moment came, and in the flames I did not freeze, I did not fail. I sprang. Finally my instinct found me. I caught it and squeezed it tight, and I hope I'll never let go.

I step into the room and close the door behind me. In the darkness I take off my clothes and lift the blanket and lie down next to my wife. Her body is warm.

Twenty-six

MEGUMI WALKS UP THE stairs to her apartment. A small plastic shopping bag imprinted with the words THANK YOU hangs from one hand. The old wooden staircase creaks with each step and she feels the grooves with her feet, worn into the steps by all those who've climbed up and down before her. Maybe she, too, over the last few years of up and down has contributed ever so slightly to the grooves in the steps. Maybe they have grown a little deeper under her weight. She has made her mark. Maybe one day someone will decide that these old grooves are too deep, too slippery, too dangerous, and will tear out the staircase and destroy her mark and replace it with a beautiful new staircase with steps perfectly straight and true and no evidence of those who came before.

Outside her open window the apple tree shimmers in the sunlight. The leaves dance gently in the breeze, rubbing together to make a soft sound. Are they waving to her? She'll miss you, apple tree. Will she once again take long walks with her father and look at the trees and the spiders in their webs? Will she be back in time for *ohanami,* to walk with her new brother among the cherry blossoms? She'll be sure to tell him about this apple tree.

The apartment is empty and soulless, stripped clear of what few possessions she had. Now it's just a box, clean and bare, a shell waiting for the next whoever. Be nice to the apple tree!

She calls for a car to the airport. "Five minutes," the dispatcher says.

In the middle of the room her suitcase stands upright. She sits on it and pulls an envelope of photographs from the THANK YOU shopping bag. Pictures from the onsen, pictures of Thomas Tessler when he had long hair, of him alone and of the two of them, faces together, smiling for the camera. Thomas once told her that every photograph tells a little white lie, but she can't help thinking those smiles were real, are real, that at that moment they were together and happy. There are pictures of him with short hair, freshly cut, her sitting on his lap. In one picture, when she thought he was looking at the camera, he was in fact looking at her. She looks closely at the expression on his face, reading it, looking for clues. His look is intense, as though he is etching her face into his memory, right down to the texture of her skin. There is no more sadness in his eyes, instead only gentle happiness and longing.

She thumbs further down the stack but then stops. Pictures of Thomas alone on the balcony, the green mountains in the background. She did not take these pictures. They are self-portraits. When did he take them? While she was in the onsen crying?

He shot the rest of the roll for her, twenty portraits, twenty different expressions, a catalog of someone she will say she once knew. She'll put her favorites on the wall, and when someone asks who it is, she'll say, "Oh, he's one of my American friends," and leave it at that, but she'll close her eyes for just a moment and remember everything, all at once, and when the feelings become too intense, unbearable, she'll open her eyes and smile.

ACKNOWLEDGMENTS

I am grateful to Amy Gash, Jae Yoon Hah, Martha Hughes, David Marshall, Elisabeth Scharlatt, and Sonoko Sugiyama.